# TENDER LOVING KITTEN CARE

"I cannot escape you, can I?" Wintergreen asked, opening his eyes and staring down at the cat. Beast's eyelids flickered in recognition, and he reached out a paw to swat lazily at Wintergreen's shoulder.

"Wonderful! Now that I am bedridden, you are moving in for the kill, are you not?" he inquired dryly. To his amazement, however, Beast did not rise to pounce upon him. Instead, he maintained his purring and burrowed against him.

"I do hope that you are comfortable, Beast. I should hate to think that I'm putting you out in any way."

"Would you like me to move him, sir?" asked Grant, easing through the door with a tray of food. "I would have done so before, but he seemed to want to sleep with you instead of me last night. My mother was sitting up with you, and she said that Beast did nothing but lie there and purr."

"Your mother sat up with me, did she?" inquired Wintergreen. "That was thoughtful of her."

# AUTUMN KITTENS

Janice Bennett
Shannon Donnelly
Mona Gedney

ZEBRA BOOKS
Kensington Publishing Corp.
http://www.zebrabooks.com

ZEBRA BOOKS are published by

Kensington Publishing Corp.
850 Third Avenue
New York, NY 10022



All Kensington titles, imprints, and distributed lines are available at special quantity discounts for bulk purchases for sales promotions, premiums, fund-raising, educational or institutional use.

Special book excerpts or customized printings can also be created to fit specific needs. For details, write or phone the office of the Kensington Special Sales Manager: Kensington Publishing Corp., 850 Third Avenue, New York, NY 10022. Attn. Special Sales Department. Phone: 1-800-221-2647.



First Printing: September 2001
10 9 8 7 6 5 4 3 2 1

Printed in the United States of America

# CONTENTS

# Inseparable

Janice Bennett

# One

Miss Ariadne Whitcombe thrust her hands deeper into her embroidered woolen muff and tramped along the wooded path, the weight of the basket over her arm reassuring rather than troubling her. A half dozen eggs, a small wheel of cheese, a loaf of fragrant, freshly baked bread, and a lidded jug of milk from the nearest farm ensured they would not go hungry this night. Tomorrow she would learn where and how to procure the supplies they would need in this unfamiliar district. Now, if only she knew for how long they would remain. . . .

The crisp October breeze sent tendrils of brown hair whipping about her chilled face. It was far too beautiful an afternoon to closet herself indoors, but she really must hurry back to the dower house to help her mother and sister with the unpacking. Of course, there wasn't that much to do, for they had placed most of their possessions into storage. She had leapt at their pressing need for provisions as an excuse to escape into the fresh air for a brisk walk. After hours spent cramped in her aunt Amabel's traveling chariot, playing such games as she could devise to divert her younger sister, Diana, this time alone was pure bliss.

A robin sang forth from the branches of an oak, to be answered by a willow warbler. The brush to the side of the path rustled, then a grouse burst forth, taking agitated wing. Three others followed in its wake. If only she could take flight, escape what would come on the morrow—

Resolutely she broke off that thought and strode forward with renewed determination. They had journeyed all this distance for a purpose. One did not find security by running away. No matter how much one wished to.

"Ari? Ari, can you hear me yet?" Diana's exasperated cry carried across the clear afternoon, causing a squirrel to scurry farther into the branches of its tree.

"I'm here!" Ari broke into a run, then slowed as the milk sloshed dangerously in its container.

In another moment the pounding of feet and the cracking of disturbed brush reached her. Then Diana, tall, slender, her long, dark curls peeping from beneath the bonnet whose apple-green ribands dangled loose, dashed headlong from behind the trees and around a bend, only to stop breathless and laughing before Ari. "Did you get everything we need?" the girl demanded, then rushed on without waiting for an answer. "Mama wants you. She cannot find where she has packed her vinaigrette, and nothing would do but I should set out after you." She turned and fell into step beside Ari.

"It is in her workbasket. I remember her putting it there distinctly, for she said that was the one place she could never lose it."

Diana wrinkled her nose. "I don't remember her looking there. She was having poor Rawlins unpack her trunks."

"Poor Rawlins, indeed. I wish we might have kept one of the footmen to do the heavy work." Ari quickened her pace, and Diana's long, easy strides kept up with her. Diana might be four years Ari's junior, but she could give her elder sister two inches in height.

Within minutes they came in sight of the elegant Georgian house, built barely sixty years previously to accommodate the imperious and exacting Dowager

Viscountess St. Clare when she decided she did not care to share a household with her equally strong-willed new daughter-in-law. The dowager, while bemoaning the possession of only six bedrooms, had promptly dragooned her son's head gardener, two of his assistants, and the undergroom to create a setting worthy of her and her new home. Four years of intensive labor produced a formal garden, the reduced scale of which was more than compensated for by the profusion of flowers laid out in their neat beds, the ornamental shrubs, and their extensive pathways. In the farthest corner of this luxurious setting stood a stable yard more than capable of housing her ladyship's three carriages, six horses, and the two grooms she insisted upon employing. In short, Ari mused as she and Diana took the shortcut through the rose garden, where the last of the year's blossoms still clung to their stems, she, Diana, and their mama had landed—at least temporarily—on their feet.

They climbed the shallow brick steps of the terrace to the accompaniment of her mother's voice, quavering with fatigue, begging Rawlins to fetch a plume to her. "What, reduced to burning feathers, Mama?" Ari demanded as they let themselves through a French window into a sitting room bathed in afternoon sunlight. "You know they always make you sneeze."

She handed the basket of provisions to Rawlins, the middle-aged woman who had been their housekeeper but was now reduced to the daunting position of their only servant. Smudges on the woman's stuff gown gave mute testimony to how hard she had labored this day. Ari gave her a grateful smile. Rawlins nodded, relinquished the feather she had just unearthed to Diana, then retreated to resume whatever occupation had been interrupted by Mrs. Whitcombe's headache. Ari strolled across to where her mother had collapsed upon a sofa, a handkerchief redolent of lavender draped over her forehead and another clutched in one hand.

Mrs. Whitcombe sat up and regarded her elder daughter in relief. "There you are at last, my love. We have been lost without you! To be sure, without you— But enough of that. You will meet your bridegroom on the morrow or the next day, as his duties permit. And how I long to see him, to see if my dear sister's description is anywhere near the mark, though I suppose we must be grateful that she has found anyone willing to marry you, positioned as you are. Not that anyone can blame you for possessing a father so improvident as to leave his estate entailed to some wretched cousin, though to be sure, he might have made some provision for us if he had tried. If only I had been able to take you to London for a Season, but there were never the funds, for it is the most shockingly expensive enterprise."

Ari, who had located the workbasket on the occasional table at her mother's side, rummaged within it, then presented her parent with the silver filigreed vinaigrette. Mrs. Whitcombe took it but did not make immediate use of this restorative. Diana, who had been idly twisting the feather between her fingers, lit it from the fire that blazed in the hearth and brought it to wave under her mother's nose.

Mrs. Whitcombe batted it away irritably, then grasped Ari's hand. "Ariadne, my love, we—poor Diana and I—rely wholly upon you. My dearest sister has been so very kind, gone to so much effort— Indeed, I dare not think what might have become of us if she had not so bestirred herself on our behalf." She eyed her elder daughter with an uneasiness bred of long experience. "You must not—you *cannot*—take one of your odd notions into your head. I am persuaded you must like Mr. Billingsworth, my love. His character must be above reproach, for he is a clergyman, and one cannot hold him to blame that he has not advanced in the church beyond a mere curate, for he has not long been ordained, though to be sure it is a pity he has neither fortune nor relatives to assist in his preferment."

"He has Uncle Geoffrey." Diana plumped down on the end of the sofa, still holding the feather.

"Do take that dreadful thing away, Diana." Mrs. Whitcombe waved her handkerchief as the acrid smoke drifted lazily into the air. "I cannot think whatever brought you to light it."

"You did, Mama," Ari said.

Mrs. Whitcombe cast her elder daughter a reproachful look, then turned back to Diana. "Your uncle Geoffrey, bless his dear, kind heart, has been persuaded to give Mr. Billingsworth the living only because of the tireless efforts of my sister."

"And only," stuck in Ari dryly, "because of *your* tireless efforts."

Mrs. Whitcombe straightened the skirts of her traveling gown. "You know perfectly well our only hope of maintaining a roof over our heads is for you to marry. We must be grateful indeed that your aunt has been able to find such an unexceptionable young gentleman, and one who is willing to take us all into his household, at that."

"Only because he can obtain a living by no other means." It cost Ari an effort to keep her voice calm. Her mother's face crumpled, and Ari sank to her knees beside the sofa. "No, dearest Mama, I promise I will not behave in some unseemly manner that will give him a disgust of me. When I meet him, I shall conduct myself with the strictest propriety."

A muffled snort sounded from the direction of Diana, and her mother regarded Ari with uneasiness. "Your dear papa always said you had an odd kick to your gallop. A most improper phrase, to be sure—"

"But very appropriate, I fear. Now, this is all the merest irritation of the nerves after our long journey.

You shall lie here quietly until Rawlins has your room ready for you, and I shall make you a cup of tea and bring you the rest of the biscuits we had in our hamper. You'll feel much more the thing in a trice." She bent forward, dropped a kiss on top of her mother's curls, signaled Diana to follow her, and left the room. As she closed the door, she had the satisfaction of seeing her mother lie back against the cushions and draw the shawl about her shoulders.

Ari made her way to the kitchen and prepared the promised tea, then saw her mother upstairs and into the apartment prepared by the overworked Rawlins. This accomplished, she turned her attention to the selection of a room for herself. She could hear Diana already unpacking her own trunk in a chamber close by. Ari peeped into each of the remaining bedrooms and chose one with a view over the back garden toward the stable. She stood for a few minutes admiring the neatly trimmed shrubs and the gray stone walls, then returned to the landing to fetch the trunk she and Diana had laboriously hauled up the stairs.

As she hung the last of her gowns in the spacious wardrobe, a deep barking erupted from outside. Curious, she crossed to the window in time to see a massive liver and white hound dashing headlong across the cobbled stones. A tiny streak of gray and white dove for the double door of the stable, squeezing through a crack at the bottom only inches ahead of its pursuer. The great hound skidded to a stop before the door, butted at the wood with its huge head, and thrust its way inside.

Before Ari realized she had moved, she was racing down the stairs. That had been a kitten, she was sure of it, and the poor thing wouldn't stand a chance against that great, vicious brute. She could reach the stable quickest through the kitchen, she decided, even before she reached the hall. Snatching up a broom that leaned against the scrubbed food-preparation table, she let herself out of the house, leaving the door swinging closed with a bang behind her.

As she ran across the kitchen garden, the barking broke off abruptly. She slowed as she reached the stable door and hefted the broom in both hands; there was, after all, a very large and dangerous-looking hound in there. But there was also a defenseless kitten. On that thought, she threw the door open wide.

Sunlight streamed in from behind her, but it didn't reach the shadowed corners of the interior. All she could see at the far end was a giant dark shape lying on top of a pile of paler straw. Her hands tightening on her weapon, she strode forward. The hound looked up at her approach, its ears pricked, its jaws parted in threat— No, they held the kitten. With a cry of horror, she rushed at it, brandishing the broom.

"What do you think you're doing?" demanded a deep, rumbling voice from behind her.

She had no time for interruptions. She brought the bristles down across the dog's muzzle, except the dog jerked back and she missed. She raised the broom again, but before a more accurate blow could fall, someone reached over her shoulder and grasped the handle, wrenching it from her hands. She spun about, furious, to glare up at a tall, dark-haired gentleman with burning brown eyes, rough-cut features, and a square jaw.

"What the devil do you mean, attacking my dog?" he demanded.

"It's got a kitten! In its mouth!" She jerked on the broom, trying to pull it free, but he held it easily with one hand.

His heavy brows rose. "Hannibal? Put it down, sir. Down." His quiet voice held only the gentlest note of command.

The hound whined, then lowered its great head and opened its massive jaws. A damp ball of gray and white fur dropped to the straw. It stood on tiny legs, shook itself vigorously, then rubbed its head against Hannibal's lower jaw. An erratic rumbling issued from the kitten's throat as the hound licked it.

Ari stared in disbelief, her arms lowering to her sides, the broom now clasped limply in her hands. Slowly, feeling rather foolish, she turned to the man who stood behind her.

"I don't believe your kitten desires to be saved," he pointed out, amusement in his voice.

His unconcerned tone infuriated her after the emotional tumult she had just undergone, and she glared at him. "It certainly ran from that hound as if in terror of its life."

"And you thought to beat it off with a broom?" The amusement increased.

She stiffened. "I wasn't about to let the poor thing be torn apart."

"Drowned, more like." He nodded to where Hannibal continued his industrious bathing of the kitten.

An idiotish look had settled over the dog's face. With one massive paw, it knocked the kitten onto its side. Ari started toward it, but the gentleman caught her by the shoulder, holding her back. Hannibal proceeded to lick the unprotesting kitten's stomach.

"He's too big," she exclaimed. "He could crush the poor little thing without realizing it."

"He's gentleness itself," her companion informed her.

"Gentle, is he? You should have seen him chasing it. You should keep him under control." She stooped down and picked up the slimy ball of fur. It regarded her with reproach.

The man's amused gaze came to rest on her face. "I had no idea I was to play landlord to a kitten. It was not mentioned that you would bring one with you. You are, by the by, one of the Misses Whitcombe? Forgive me for not calling upon you formally. I have only just arrived myself."

"You are St. Clare!" She regarded him with much the horror she had just regarded his disreputable hound. Fear raced through her that she might have offended their host, might have made him regret extending the hospitality of his dower house to her family. She knew very little about him, about his temperament, just that her aunt Amabel considered this cousin of her husband's to be a trifle eccentric and that he had recently become engaged.

He gave a slight bow. "Allow me to welcome you to the Grange. I hope you had a pleasant journey?"

"Yes," she managed to say. Then, "The kitten isn't ours. The first time I saw it was when your dog chased it into the stable." She caught the defensive note in her voice and straightened, cradling the squirming kitten close.

The hound clambered to its oversized paws and pressed against her leg. It lowered itself to its haunches, still leaning against her, and tilted its head up to gaze longingly at the kitten.

"Hannibal," Viscount St. Clare said softly. He snapped his fingers, and the dog shifted its great bulk from her side to his. The gaze never left the kitten. "So you are Amabel Sommersby's niece," he said, regarding her critically. "There is little resemblance between you."

"True," said Ari. "She is a great beauty. How kind of you to point out the dissimilarity." At that, his generous mouth broke into a wide grin, causing her heart to lurch in an extremely agreeable manner. Heavens, he was attractive. His fiancée must count herself extremely lucky.

Hannibal rose on his hind legs, his gigantic muzzle reaching for the kitten clutched in Ari's arms. "Stop it!" she ordered, drawing back.

"He won't hurt it," St. Clare assured her.

"You can't know that." She lifted the kitten beyond

the hound's reach. "He might not be vicious, but his idea of playing could crush something this small."

If anything, St. Clare's amusement increased. "He won't," he said simply.

Ari glared at him, indignant that the man would so casually dismiss her fears. "The kitten does not belong to you?" she demanded, her tones chilly.

"It does not."

"Then I shall take it where it can be safe." With that, she awarded him a dismissive nod and strode out of the stable.

# Two

Ari's anger with St. Clare carried her half the distance to the dower house before it occurred to her that her mother might not appreciate this addition to their household. She paused in the kitchen garden, hugging the purring kitten close. No, no matter what anyone said, she would keep this poor little thing safe. And if this curate her aunt had found for her disliked cats? She shivered at the thought. She must marry him whatever he was like. Yet how could she live in a household devoid of felines? Or with a man who could harden his heart to the plight of tiny, innocent creatures?

She resumed walking, but slowly, her fingers caressing the little ears. She was in no position to demand perfection from her proposed husband. She needed to secure her family's future the only way she could, which was through this marriage arranged by her mother's only sister. It was so very good of dear aunt Amabel to go to so much trouble, to unearth this poor curate for her.

He must be as desperate as she to make an honorable way through the world. She could only hope his poverty was the worst there was to know of him. What his character might be like— Well, he was a man of the cloth. That, at least, must imply some measure of intelligence and goodwill. She would have to wait until she actually met him to know whether he was possessed of sense or kindliness or humor.

Thought of humor brought St. Clare uncomfortably to mind. Would her curate possess rugged features and sparkling, laughing eyes? She doubted it. It was hard to imagine anyone else endowed with these gifts to the same disconcerting degree as the viscount. But perhaps he would hold more sensible views on the subject of tiny kittens and massive hounds. She must hope so. And it would be so very agreeable if he also possessed a smile that could warm her heart. . . .

She thrust her nonsensical romantic notions aside, for she was not one to dwell on regrets. She would meet this curate on the morrow with the hope and intention of being pleased. If she could find but one trait, one characteristic she could admire in him, she would be satisfied. She would also, a little voice murmured within her, be relieved.

A vision of Viscount St. Clare's dancing eyes returned to haunt her. With a vexed exclamation, she set off to find some occupation to drive that irritating gentleman from her mind.

A great many tasks awaited her, with the result she had little leisure to reflect upon the possible nature of her proposed bridegroom, or upon the enticing qualities of the viscount, until she at last slipped between sheets late that night. The kitten, named Sappho by Diana, had been accepted into the household with no more than a distracted protest from her mother, which the sisters easily overbore. Ari had placed a basket for it beside her bed, but no sooner had she drawn the coverlet to her chin than she heard the unmistakable sound of pin-sharp kitten claws coming to grips with fabric. The coverlets tugged to one side, and a moment later the triumphant Sappho stalked across the bedding and settled down to sleep just beneath Ari's chin.

She scooped the kitten into her hands, rolled to her

side, and cradled her purring companion while she considered the events of the day—and those of the morrow. Exhaustion took its toll, and within minutes she had drifted into sleep, from which she was roused at last only by the kitten's imperious mewing and a soft batting at her nose. Ari dragged open her eyes to discover the sunlight flooding through the partly open rose-patterned curtains and spilling across the great bedstead. She stretched, detached Sappho from the ruffle at her wrist, and set the kitten on the floor, where it promptly attacked one of her slippers. Tending to the kitten's needs, dressing herself, and straightening the room managed to occupy her so that she blocked out her worries until it was time for breakfast.

As she left her room, Diana emerged from the one next door, sleepy-eyed and stretching. "I have never done so much heavy work in my life!" the girl declared, then added, "Good morning, dear one," and scooped the unprotesting Sappho from Ari's arm. After a moment, the girl looked up, her expression serious. "Do you think he will come today?" There was no need to say whom she meant by "he." As far as the Whitcombe ladies were concerned, no other gentleman existed aside from the Reverend Mr. Billingsworth.

Ari tickled the kitten behind the ear. "I doubt he knows we have arrived. And as we can hardly send him a note to inform him, we shall have to wait until one or another of his parishioners mentions the matter to him."

Diana regarded her uncertainly. "You will like him excessively, Ari. You must."

"Yes," Ari agreed. "I must."

They fell silent as they made their way down the stairs. In the hall they paused, but enticing aromas drifted from the east side of the house, and they followed their noses to a sun-filled breakfast chamber hung with lace curtains and filled with elegant dark wood furnishings. Silver gleamed on the table at which their mother sat, addressing a slice of ham.

Ari stopped, staring at it. "I did not get that at the farm yesterday."

"No, my love. The viscount has been ever so gracious. He sent a kitchen maid across with a basket brimming with food. I hope he will pay us a morning visit so we may thank him properly. He even," she added, "sent a pitcher of cream especially for your kitten."

"Did he?" Ari busied herself at the sideboard to hide the soft flush that crept across her cheeks. "It was probably an apology for allowing that wretched hound of his to trample the poor thing."

"Ari—" Her mother broke off. "You are not going to take one of your dislikes to him, are you? When he has been so very good as to allow us to rent the dower house, and for so very little, simply because his cousin married my sister. We are greatly in his debt, for there is no other way that you could meet Mr. Billingsworth, and he has been so kind, so thoughtful to send us this excellent ham."

"No, Mama." Ari managed a bright smile for her parent. "I did not take him in dislike. He is indeed the gentleman, though perhaps he allows his odd humors to get the better of him at times."

"That? From you?" Diana hooted in a most unladylike manner, drawing down protests from her doting mama.

They had barely finished breakfast, when the sound of hooves on the gravel drive reached them. Diana sprang from her chair and ran to the window. "It is a gentleman," she called over her shoulder.

"Is it the viscount?" her mama asked quickly. She rose, looking helplessly about the scattered plates on the table.

Diana leaned to one side. "He is wearing a black

coat. No," she added the next moment. "I can see his collar. He is a clergyman."

Ari's stomach dropped abruptly, doing unpleasant things to the breakfast of ham and eggs she had just consumed.

"Oh, my love." Mrs. Whitcombe cast a dismayed glance over Ari. "There is no time to change your gown. If you will but straighten your hair!" She patted at it over Ari's protests, dislodging the previously neat arrangement of curls.

"He is riding around the back!" called Diana.

Ari gently set her mother aside. "He will be putting his horse in the stable. What—what does he look like?"

"Sloping shoulders, sturdy legs. A bay," pronounced Diana with the mischievous smile that said quite clearly she had deliberately misunderstood her sister's aching question.

"Beast," said Ari with forced cheerfulness. "Does Mr. Billingsworth look the gentleman?"

Diana considered a moment. "He does," she said at last. "And he looks every bit as terrified as do you."

"Pray do not put any such ideas into her head. Ariadne, my love, you look very well. Now, let us go into the morning room. No, run upstairs and fetch your stitchery. You must not have him think you idle. Run, girl. There is little time."

Ari found herself thrust out the door. Followed by her mother's urgings, she hurried up the stairs, fetched her working basket, and returned before her fretting mama had gone quite distracted. Diana propelled her into a chair near the open window, took another at her side, then jumped up and changed positions so as to leave this one free for their guest. Ari drew out the topmost item from her mending, discovered it to be a chemise, and hastily thrust it out of sight. The single flounce on her sprigged muslin morning gown would be far more suitable. She had barely picked up her needle and set the first stitch, when a knock sounded on the door.

"He has a firm hand," Diana said in the voice of one determined to find as many pleasing qualities in their visitor as possible. "Very direct."

Ari made no reply. A wave of nervous nausea swept through her.

A very few minutes passed, then Rawlins's familiar short, plump figure opened the door, and the woman announced in her habitual calm, matter-of-fact tones, "The Reverend Mr. Billingsworth, madam."

A young man who could be no more than six-and-twenty stood on the threshold, garbed as a clergyman, his hat clenched tightly in one fist. He stood just above the average height, with a well-proportioned figure and an amiable countenance. Not precisely handsome, Ari decided, but far from displeasing. His erratic sandy hair curled at odd angles, giving him the appearance of a mischievous schoolboy.

He gave one quick glance about, then focused on Ari's mother. He advanced into the room a cautious step. "Mrs. Whitcombe? I am Thaddeus Billingsworth. Forgive me for presenting myself so soon after your arrival, but—but I desired to be among the first to welcome you to the neighborhood."

Mrs. Whitcombe's broad smile seemed quite genuine. She rose gracefully to her feet and advanced a step to meet him, holding out her hand. He took it, then after a moment's hesitation carried it to his lips before releasing it. Mrs. Whitcombe beamed on him. "My dear sir, how very kind, how very considerate of you to call, for you must know we are quite out of our depth here and have not the slightest notion to whom we should turn for advice on any matter. Tradesmen," she added as he merely stared at her, his eyes glazing over with a panicky expression.

"Tradesmen. To be sure. Tradesmen." He relaxed, apparently on sure ground. "Of course. You must be in need of any number of things." His gaze strayed to Diana, then on to Ariadne. He swallowed and turned back to her mother. "I hope you had a pleasant journey."

"Indeed, we could not help but be a little anxious—" She broke off under Ari's furious glare. "Though to be sure, that is neither here nor there. It was most pleasant, for my dear sister sent her own traveling chariot to convey us here, and her groom saw to everything. But we must not be standing here. Will you not be seated?"

Mr. Billingsworth looked wildly about, but the only vacant chair was the one Diana had left next to Ari. Offering her an uncertain smile, he took it.

Mrs. Whitcombe beamed even brighter. "You must allow me to present my daughters. Miss Whitcombe, and Miss Diana Whitcombe."

Mr. Billingsworth sprang at once to his feet and bowed low over Ari's hand. As he turned to Diana, a deep flush showed across his countenance. As soon as he regained his chair, he positioned himself to face Mrs. Whitcombe again. "I hope you found all to your liking here? I believe the viscount is expected shortly—"

"He arrived last evening, shortly after we did ourselves." Mrs. Whitcombe looked up as the door opened and Rawlins staggered in under the weight of a laden tray. The curate sprang up once more, taking it from the servant's hands and placing it on the table. "How kind." Mrs. Whitcombe cast a pointed look at Ari. "My dear, will you not pour a glass of wine for Mr. Billingsworth?"

The refreshments provided a safe topic of conversation, and Ari found herself able to ask the gentleman's preference with no more than the slightest stammer. When she had exhausted her abilities to discuss the contents of the tray, she found herself floundering. He came to her aid by praising the fine weather and their good fortune in having avoided a promised storm. Her tentative question about local points of interest brought the first genuine smile to his lips, and this saw them through the correct half-hour of his visit. He rose promptly, thanked them for his gracious reception, and took himself off about his various parish duties. Mrs. Whitcombe dispatched Ari to escort him to the door, but as he did no more than thank her again before striding toward the stable, little was accomplished by this ploy.

As soon as Ari returned to the room, Diana swooped down on her and embraced her. "It is the greatest relief!" cried the younger girl. "Oh, Ari, he is not in the least dreadful. His manners are most pleasing."

"I was quite struck by his innate goodness," declared Mrs. Whitcombe. "His conversation was marked by sincerity, and I thought his comments showed thought and intelligence. Oh, my dear Ariadne, I could not be happier. He seems a most excellent young gentleman."

"Indeed, he does," Ari agreed in a rather flat voice.

Mrs. Whitcombe stared at her, aghast. "My love, you must have liked him. There was nothing about him not to like."

"No, indeed." She managed a shaky smile. "Only he has so many good qualities, I fear he must be vividly aware that I have not."

The fear that she was not good enough to be the wife of such an earnest, diligent young man of the cloth haunted her, especially since he was possessed of so gentle and kindly a disposition. She knew her own temper to be uneven, and that she possessed a reprehensible streak of quirkishness that a clergyman might find unsuitable in his life's companion. Yet even though he was being coerced into this union every bit as much as she, he certainly seemed to be trying to make the best of it. All in all, she told herself, she was luckier than she deserved.

Of course, she didn't yet know what he thought of kittens.

With her mother and sister praising Mr. Billingsworth and making plans for a wedding and life to follow, Ari quickly found the atmosphere in the morning room to be insupportable. They didn't seem to need her in the least to assist in their raptures. She slipped out the door, ran up to her room for her pelisse, then down to the kitchen, where Sappho hung off Rawlins's apron, much to the housekeeper's annoyance. Taking the kitten with her, Ari set forth on a long, rambling walk.

For some time the kitten seemed content to nestle in the crook of her arm and look around or tug at the woolen scarf she had wrapped around her head. Finally it jumped free of her hold and dashed about, looking under bushes and behind branches, leaping into the air and batting at anything that moved. Ari strolled on, watching the kitten as it played or ran to catch up to her.

She felt no better than she had the day before, she realized in dismay as she at last turned back to the house. She ought to. Mr. Billingsworth might have proved to possess any number of disagreeable qualities. Instead, the only possible fault she could find in him was a tendency toward seriousness that did not match her own love of the ridiculous.

And what was he thinking of her? Was he regretting the circumstances that obliged him to offer for her? Was he relieved that she was not as bad as he might have feared? That possibility brought a wry smile to her lips. She was not the only one coerced by the needs of family to agree to this match. He, too, had a mother in need of support, and a younger brother still at Cambridge. No, a mere curate could never hope to support a hopeful young gentleman at that institution. He needed his vicarage.

The snapping of branches and the crashing of a

large body moving at speed through the underbrush brought her up short. Moments later, the giant Hannibal burst onto the path, lunging for Sappho. The kitten raced for the safety of Ari's skirts, and the hound tore after it, slamming into her, knocking her from her feet. She sprawled on the ground, felt the kitten scramble over her, using its needle-sharp claws for traction, then a wave of vile breath preceded a rough and ready licking of her face. Hannibal, it seemed, was delighted to find her on his own level.

She struggled up to one elbow, trying to fend off the hound's eager greeting. Somewhere nearby she heard a whistle, but she was too busy trying to preserve her skirts from the muddy paws to pay it much heed. Branches cracked, there was a moment of silence, then St. Clare's voice, struggling with laughter, called, "Hannibal! Stop that, sir. Come here."

The hound bounded to his master, panting, his dripping tongue lolling, and the viscount scratched him casually behind the ears. Ari glared at the man, who seemed to be deriving far too much entertainment from, and far too little concern over, her plight.

He strode to her side, holding out his hand. "Allow me to help you."

Ari gathered herself together and accepted his aid as the most dignified method of regaining her feet. The clasp on her hand was firm, his strength noticeable as he drew her easily from the ground. A surprisingly pleasant experience, all things considered. She felt her cheeks warm from awareness of him. To cover her confusion, she said, "That hound is a menace."

Hannibal, apparently taking this as a compliment, lunged toward her with a joyous bark, knocking her against the viscount. She collided against his broad chest, encountering solid muscle beneath her hand as she caught her balance against him. His arm swept about her, steadying her, and she found herself staring at his smooth-scraped square chin. An elusive, appealing scent hung about him, which might have been West Indian bay rum.

This was far too unsettling. She pulled away. "Can you not keep that dreadful dog under control?" she demanded. "He is dangerously rough."

But at that moment, despite the fact Hannibal held down the kitten with one massive paw and licked it, little Sappho purred.

Ari regarded the furry pair in irritation. "That rather takes a great deal of force from my words." St. Clare laughed, and she transferred her glare to him. "It is all well and good for you to laugh now, but what about next time? That great beast could seriously hurt so tiny a kitten. Or a fair-sized lion, for that matter."

"If you were to keep it indoors," he suggested, "there would be no chance of any harm coming to it."

She started to give a scathing reply, but the recollection that this was his property and she only a tenant caused her to shut it again. Bidding him a cold good morning, she scooped up the kitten and stalked off. The sound of his deep chuckle followed her, as tantalizing as it was annoying.

# Three

Ari swung the basket that dangled from her hand as she drew in deep breaths of the crisp autumn air. At her side, Diana sighed, the sound one of pure contentment. The lane was smooth and well kept, bordered by ditches that gave way to a wide grass verge with tall hawthorn shrubs on one side and a line of ancient beeches and scattered oaks on the other. Ari felt free, freer than she had in ages, freer than she might ever feel again.

She slammed shut the door on thoughts of her impending marriage, of the necessary decorum she must display as the wife of a clergyman. She wasn't one yet, and she would make the most of it while she could. She glanced sideways at Diana, who studied the topmost branches of the trees, probably searching for the squirrel or bird that caused the faint scrabbling noises.

"See that stump?" Ari demanded. "Just where the lane bends? I'll race you."

With a whoop, Diana broke into a run, leaving Ari to scramble after her. Diana's legs might be the longer, but Ari caught her up halfway to their goal, snatched the scarf that hung loose about her sister's neck, and veered away, leaping the ditch. Diana, laughing, set off in pursuit. Ari passed the stump, not wanting to stop yet. Turning to face her sister, she danced around the bend in the lane, waving the scarf above her head like a banner. Diana rounded the corner after her and stopped abruptly, her expression sobering. Half suspecting this to be a ruse to catch her, Ari continued backward, though slower.

"Ari—" Diana grimaced and gestured for Ari to turn around.

Ari stopped, her joy in the beauty of the morning sinking beneath sudden foreboding. Lowering the scarf, she looked over her shoulder.

The Reverend Mr. Billingsworth stood ten yards away, his face somber as his gaze rested on her.

Well, she would have to brazen this out. "Good morning, Mr. Billingsworth," she called. "It is the loveliest day, is it not?"

"Indeed it is, Miss Whitcombe." He didn't smile. "Good morning, Miss Diana."

Diana came to Ari's side and retrieved her scarf from her sister's limp grasp. "Good morning, sir." Her eyes held a guarded, worried look.

"Are you going to the village?" A touch of austerity that hadn't been present on the previous day colored his voice.

Probably, Ari reflected, because she had behaved in a proper manner, then. She could not forget this poor man was being pressured into marrying her. He knew little about her, but he knew a great deal about the position she would be required to fill. Warmth touched her cheeks and she looked down, knowing she had disappointed him.

"We are going to see what vegetables are available," Diana announced brightly, filling the stretching silence.

"Then allow me to escort you. I know the very place." Mr. Billingsworth offered Ari his arm.

She took it but kept her gaze lowered with what she hoped was a becoming show of modesty as she fell into step with him. If he must marry her, and she him, she would try to be a good and proper wife, but crisp autumn mornings cried out for laughter and races, not solemn strolls. A clergyman, of course, could never so far forget his dignity as to join in any such foolish game. She forced back her regrets; she knew her duty and would not shirk it.

"Is this a large parish?" she asked, and had the satisfaction of seeing a measure of animation enter the man's face as he launched onto the topic of the various troubles currently besetting his flock. He was a good man, she reflected; they had been right in their estimation of his character the day before. A trifle serious for her taste, but then, his was not a frivolous calling. He was admirably suited to his chosen task.

And she? She was woefully inadequate.

Did he think so? She peeped up sideways at him, then away at once. He must think so. Well, she would simply have to strive harder to be worthy of him. Perhaps, if she entered into his concerns for his parishioners, if she concentrated very hard on behaving with the strictest propriety most of the time, he might forgive her less dignified moments.

Mr. Billingsworth escorted them to a tiny cottage on the outskirts of the village, the home of a widow, he informed them. Hers was not the typical garden of roses and vines, but neatly tended vegetable beds. "She will be glad to supplement her meager income," the curate assured Ari as they approached the door.

Their purchases made, Mr. Billingsworth apologized for not being able to escort them home once more, but his business would keep him among his flock for some little time. Ari thanked him for his aid, they took their leave, and started back toward the dower house.

"He is a very good sort of gentleman," Diana said after a few minutes.

"Yes." Ari tried to keep the bleakness out of her voice. "He is."

"One must honor him for his kindness," Diana pursued in the tones of one trying to convince herself.

Ari slipped her arm about her sister's waist and gave her a quick hug. "I am very lucky," she said. "Beyond what I deserve. And once he has gained his living, and assured the well-being of his own family, perhaps he will smile more often."

As they walked back along the lane, hoofbeats sounded from behind, overtaking them rapidly. They stepped to the side as a neat curricle pulled by a pair of chestnuts swept up to them. A gentleman of middle years in a many-caped driving coat and high-crowned beaver held the ribands. At his side sat a rather pretty girl with a gentle expression, eyes downcast. She glanced at Ari and Diana with interest, then they were past, bowling along at a spanking pace.

"That's the way to travel," sighed Diana. "We'll be lucky to have a gig, I suppose."

Ari's lips twitched. "We'll be thankful to have one, you mean. Is that not the opening in the hedge that is our shortcut?" she added, and hurried ahead to check.

It was, and it led them across the park and to the kitchen entrance of the dower house. Ari handed her basket over to the waiting Rawlins, who examined the vegetables with a knowledgeable eye. Nodding in satisfaction, the woman whisked the basket away to the pantry.

A plaintive mewing demanded Ari's attention, and she stooped to pick up Sappho, who had been rubbing her head against Ari's ankle. Still holding the purring kitten, she followed Diana into the morning room, where their mother sat frowning over the bonnet she attempted to decorate.

Mrs. Whitcombe looked up, smiling. "You missed the arrival, my love. St. Clare has visitors! I cannot be certain, of course, but I cannot imagine it could be anyone other than his fiancée and her papa."

"I believe we saw them!" cried Diana. "A girl with dark curls, in the most ravishing pelisse and fur muff? They passed us in the lane."

Ari sank onto a chair, picked up a discarded piece of riband, and dangled it in front of the kitten. It batted at it, then hunkered down to pounce. So that had been St. Clare's fiancée. A lovely girl, so very well bred. Ari couldn't image *her* playing boisterous games in a public place. She had seemed so very proper, a perfect viscountess.

So why did it bother her? She had known since before she met him that St. Clare was engaged. To feel any regret was foolishness. She herself was engaged—at least, she would be once her prospective bridegroom brought himself up to scratch and offered for her. And he would, because he had as little choice in the matter as she. So what St. Clare did, and whom he chose to marry, was no concern of hers.

Still, and quite uncharacteristically, she found for herself chores that kept her within doors, and out of the way of any chance meetings, for the better part of the day.

Not until the kitten's pointed mewing could not be ignored did she at last abandon her detested mending and take the little creature to the kitchen to find it some milk and scraps of meat. There she found Rawlins chopping vegetables. A splendid salmon lay on the sideboard, a pile of potatoes at its side.

Rawlins looked up at her entrance, and with the back of one hand brushed from her eyes the stray hairs that had escaped from her mobcap. "Is anyone to deliver milk today, Miss Ari?" she asked. "For if they are, I hope they'll be quick about it. I want to get a sauce on the simmer."

"Milk," Ari repeated. "Oh, dear. I forgot to make arrangements. I'll see what I can do," she added hastily at the housekeeper's harassed expression. She found a remnant of cheese for Sappho, grasped the pitcher, and while the kitten concentrated on eating, Ari slipped out the door.

"Try up at the manor house, miss," called Rawlins after her. "Cook said we could get anything we needed from her."

Ari hesitated. She didn't want to go near the Grange, where St. Clare entertained his fiancée and her father. But it would take almost an hour longer to go to the farm. Comforting herself with the conviction that neither St. Clare nor his guests were likely to venture anywhere near the kitchens, she set forth across the yard and to the path that led through the wood.

She had been right. The viscount was not in the kitchens. He was in his stable yard, and that proved every bit as bad, for her path led right past it. She started to turn away, to circle around the yard and approach the kitchen through its garden, but he raised a hand, acknowledging her, and she had no choice but to join him and his party.

Hannibal, who had been snuffling about the loose boxes, pricked his ears at the scuff of her slippers on the cobbled stones and bounded to greet her. She held the pitcher above her head, taking the brunt of his overpowering welcome against her knees and her free hand, and she stumbled backward a pace from the impact.

"Hannibal!" St. Clare called, and the giant hound dropped to his haunches, tongue lolling to one side, an expression of idiotish delight on his face.

"Yes, I am pleased to see you too," she told the disreputable animal, holding him off from drooling on her gown. "Yes, sir. Good boy."

"Hannibal!" St. Clare repeated, snapping his fingers at his side. The hound heaved himself once more to his massive paws and ambled over to lean against his master's leg. "Miss Whitcombe," St. Clare went on somewhat stiffly. "Allow me to present you to Sir William Allingham and his daughter, Miss Allingham."

The gentleman raised his hat, revealing a balding pate fringed by graying brown hair. His expression remained cool. Ari acknowledged his bow with a slight curtsy, then turned to the daughter. Pretty, indeed, with a sweet face and gentle green eyes, and a warmth entirely lacking in her parent.

Miss Allingham acknowledged the introduction with shy pleasure. Those large eyes regarded Ari with a tentative, hopeful expression. "How delightful to have someone of my own age in the neighborhood," she said with a trembling smile. "I—I feel certain we must become fast friends. I should like it of all things."

The sincerity of the words took Ari aback. It was rare to encounter so much genuine warmth. Society as a whole was so artificial, the members of the *ton* exchanging veiled insults through false smiles. But no artifice existed in this girl. "I hope so, indeed," Ari found herself saying, for she realized with surprise that she would like this girl for a friend. There was nothing not to like about her—except that she was engaged to St. Clare.

And she could understand the viscount choosing her. The girl would make an excellent viscountess, her manners correct, her demeanor always above reproach. She would look after the people of his estate, who would undoubtedly love her.

But when next she met Miss Allingham, Ari could only hope St. Clare would not be at hand. She found his presence disturbing, and in a manner that was wholly inappropriate since they were both engaged to others. "I must not keep you," she said abruptly. "Our poor housekeeper is most eager for some milk." She made a vague gesture with the pitcher.

"Ask my cook for anything you need," St. Clare invited.

Ari thanked him and made the mistake of raising her gaze to his face. She looked away again quickly. He was infuriating, she reminded herself as she strode toward the manor. He allowed that ridiculous hound to maul her poor Sappho and acted as if there were nothing amiss. That ought to be enough to make her dislike him. Yet her pulse raced and the strangest longings stirred in her heart whenever she saw him.

Dwelling on such ridiculous fancies was the outside of enough! she scolded herself. He was engaged. And so would she soon be. Poor Mr. Billingsworth was in no position to be deterred by her many flaws.

She left the manor house at last with not only the required milk but also a basket of eggs and several tart apples that St. Clare's housekeeper, Mrs. Flint, assured her would make an excellent tart. To Ari's relief, St. Clare and his party were no longer in the stable. He must have been seeing them off, she reflected, then forced her mind to the subject of slicing apples and begging sufficient sugar from their limited store to make the treat.

The following morning, Mrs. Whitcombe hurried into the breakfast room after both her daughters had nearly finished their meal. She clasped a tray of rolls in her hands, and she beamed with all the air of one bearing news. "Well," she declared as she placed the fragrant bread on the sideboard. "I have learned all about her. Mrs. Flint, who is housekeeper for St. Clare, brought bacon over to us herself, and I was quite beside myself to discover why, when she could far more easily have sent one of the servants, and then I realized she wanted to talk about this Miss Allingham. It seems St. Clare has known her since she was in her cradle, and always the sweetest and gentlest child, and they played together, the three of them, St. Clare and Miss Allingham and St. Clare's brother, who was killed at Waterloo last spring. Mrs. Flint thinks it must have been his brother's dying that made St. Clare think to marry at last, and to choose his childhood friend. So very romantic, do you not think?"

Diana looked skeptical. "Sweet and gentle? From what you've said, Ari, it sounds as if St. Clare is of a more lively disposition."

"He is," Ari agreed. "Which is why he might prefer a gentle girl. And she is, you know, for I met her briefly yesterday. I do not see how he could help but love her." She herself would do well to study the girl's manners and emulate them. She could not help but feel Mr. Billingsworth would be relieved by such a change in her.

She had returned to the distasteful but necessary chore of mending, when it occurred to her that no kitten aided her by chewing on her thread or filching delicate garments from her basket. Surprised at this desertion by her faithful companion, she went in search of Sappho. The kitchen seemed the most likely place, but no sign of the little feline did she see. She asked Rawlins, who was stacking dishes on a shelf.

"Slipped outside about an hour ago, Miss Ari," the woman told her. "As bent on a lark as ever you have been. I daresay she'll be ready to come back in by now."

Ari, feeling it was time whether the kitten thought so or not, set forth in search of her.

Sappho did not seem to have sprawled herself for a nap in any of the patches of late morning sun. She might be anywhere, of course, chasing squirrels or teasing birds, but Ari headed for the stable, where the kitten would be able to chase, even if not catch, mice. As soon as she stepped inside the stone structure, even before her eyes adjusted to the sudden darkness, she heard rustlings.

"Sappho?" she called. "Where are you?" She advanced, focusing on the noises, to the opening of one of the loose boxes. Straw lay strewn thick across the floor, fresh and sweet-smelling, as if it awaited an occupant. The kitten bounded through it, burrowing deep, then leaping high to pounce on an unsuspecting wisp. Amused, Ari leaned back against the stall partition to watch.

The sudden scrabbling of claws on the cobbles outside provided her only warning. The next moment the graceless, boisterous Hannibal burst through the open door, charged across the stone floor, and romped into the straw in pursuit of Sappho. With a cry of dismay, Ari lunged after him, trying to grab him about the neck, to pull him away from his quarry. The hound spared her a joyous lick that caught her square across the face and butted against her so she fell to her knees. Sappho sat back, hissing, swatting at the massive paws that threatened to squash her. Ari dove for the kitten, grasping it around its middle just as Hannibal flopped his great weight to the ground and rolled over, kicking straw into the air as he worked his back into the scratchy pile.

"Do you know," came St. Clare's drawling voice from somewhere behind her, "you look perfectly demented. No, pray, do not take that wisp from across your face. You will quite spoil the effect."

Indignation swelled within her. She pulled what straw she could from her hair as she turned to glare at him. "Can you not keep this wretched beast of yours under control? I have never known anyone less fit to have the charge of an animal than you, forever permitting it to run wild and terrorize little creatures."

St. Clare, to her utter disgust, grinned, his eyes dancing with unholy enjoyment. "And be deprived of such sights as this?"

"If you were a gentleman, you would rescue me from this hound." He had no right to set her pulse racing, especially when he laughed at her. Yet he did, which played havoc with her anger.

"No, the rescuing of damsels in distress is the job of knights errant. A gentleman"—and he stepped forward, holding out his hand—"overlooks the impropriety of a young lady's behaving like a sad romp.'

She froze, outraged, then burst into laughter. "You are abominable, sir, and no gentleman." She allowed him to assist her to her feet, handed him the protesting kitten, and left him to fend off Hannibal while she set about straightening her hair. The next moment Sappho sprang free, burrowing once more in the hay, with Hannibal in joyous pursuit.

"Oh, do get out of here!" she exclaimed, exasperated. "Take that dreadful hound of yours, or I shall never be able to rescue poor Sappho. She will never emerge as long as you and that idiotish animal of yours remain anywhere near."

"Nonsense. Hannibal!" He snapped his fingers, calling the dog to heel.

To Ari's mingled annoyance and relief, the hound gave off digging in the straw and came to St. Clare's side.

"You are as exasperating as your master," Ari informed the panting hound.

"Are you going to burrow farther into the hay?" St. Clare inquired, his eyes still laughing at her. "You'll do even more damage to your gown."

The flounce of her skirt had torn, she realized, and a vexed exclamation escaped her. "It is all your fault!" she declared. "And I detest needlework of all things, and it is all I have done since arriving here! Oh, do go away, you and Hannibal have done quite enough damage."

A sound by the door interrupted her before she could add any more reproofs. She spun about to look over St. Clare's shoulder, and her heart sank as she saw Mr. Billingsworth standing in the opening, watching and listening, a look of concerned dismay on his normally amiable features.

# Four

Ari swallowed and stared helplessly at the curate. Not for anything would she have had him see her like this. To think she had resolved only that morning to try to model her behavior upon that of Miss Allingham. And now, the very first time she saw him again, she was behaving as badly as ever. Her hand crept to the torn ruffle at her sleeve in an attempt to cover it, but she knew it was too late. Vividly, she was aware she proved herself unsuitable to be his wife and could not blame him if he could not bring himself to go through with this devil's bargain her aunt had created.

And Ari would have no one but herself to blame when she, her mother, and Diana found themselves with no home and no means to command the necessities of life.

A long, awkward moment of silence followed. At last, Ari managed to say, "Good morning, Mr. Billingsworth. I—" She found herself completely at a loss for words.

Mr. Billingsworth strode forward, drawing with him a bay hack. "I came to stable my mount before paying a call upon your mother," he said with commendable ease. "I see you are having some difficulty. Is there any way in which I might be of service to you?"

What a dear, good man, Ari reflected, more miserably aware than ever of how she must fail to meet his standards. She could see in his face how she had disappointed him once again. Such a look of misgiving. And she couldn't blame him in the least. Why couldn't she be the sensible, gentle wife he needed? Why couldn't Aunt Amabel simply have her husband give him the living without taking her, Ari, as well?

Because this was the only way Aunt Amabel could look after her family, Ari knew. It was not just this poor curate she must be disappointing, but her mother and sister and aunt too, if they only knew how reprehensibly she had behaved.

St. Clare filled the silence that had begun to stretch uncomfortably. "You will be of far more assistance than I," he said. "Miss Whitcombe, allow me to apologize for the deplorable behavior of Hannibal." The dog grinned foolishly at her, his tongue hanging out the side of his mouth. "I shall remove him from the scene, and then perhaps you may rescue your kitten without our further interference." He sketched a bow to her and, still grasping Hannibal by the generous scruff of his neck, led him away.

Mr. Billingsworth watched the viscount's departure, then turned back to Ari. "Is the kitten injured?" he asked in concerned tones.

"No," Ari said quickly. "She is the quickest little thing. Only the dog is so very huge—" The kitten chose that moment to stick its gray and white nose out from beneath a pile of straw.

"Ah," said Mr. Billingsworth, a slight smile touching his lips at last. "Unless I am much mistaken, there is your quarry now."

Ari scooped the little ball of fur into her hands, then realized Mr. Billingsworth waited for her to exit the loose box. As soon as she had stepped outside, he led his mount within, fastened it with a head collar, and set about unbuckling the girth. Ari, well aware she had already damaged her gown, picked up some straw and scraped the animal's damp back.

"You are very kind to animals," said the curate in the tones of one determined to find some good in her, and hitting upon the only hope.

It proved too much for Ari. She turned to face him, the straw dangling from one hand, the squirming kitten clutched close against her side with the other. "I do most sincerely apologize," she said, "but I fear we must speak frankly with each other. We are both fully aware of our situation and how dreadfully awkward it is. Please, you must not feel constrained to offer for me if you feel I will not suit." She lowered her gaze, staring at Sappho, unable to meet the curate's steady regard. "I—I fear I am quite desperately unsuitable for the role of a vicar's wife. You must not consider my position. As a man of the cloth, you have greater responsibilities to your future flock." She heard him draw in a deep breath and braced herself.

He didn't speak at once though. He was silent for a long while, then seemed at last to come to a decision. "I do know your position full well, and I understand perfectly why you must consider marriage with a gentleman who must seem lamentably dull to you."

Ari flushed. "It is no such thing."

He held up a hand, silencing her, a sad smile still tugging at his lips. "Has your aunt explained my situation to you?"

Ari nodded. "A brother at Cambridge and a widowed mother to provide for. No, I quite see. You are trapped into this, no matter how little it may be to your taste. I must suppose you have examined all other alternatives." She made it a statement, not a question.

His smile became a trifle less forced. "I fear I have no connections and no prospects. Livings are few and far between."

"But if you truly fear I am unsuitable, my aunt cannot hold you to this bargain. I could write to her and tell her, and surely she could not blame you for my erratic temperament."

He studied her upturned face. "Your concern for my future flock, at the risk to your own security, proves the goodness of your heart. But we need make no irrevocable decisions as yet. I must admit, at the moment this does seem the best solution for us both."

She swallowed. "I promise I shall try very hard to become more suitable."

She kept her promise throughout that day and most of the next, until the beauty of the weather lured her away from her chores, outdoors and across the parkland, where the wild creatures busied themselves preparing for winter. Squirrels scampered from branch to branch, and her heart played with them among the trees. When she at last returned from this illicit expedition, guiltily later than she had intended, it was to be met by her mother with the excited intelligence that they had been invited to dine with Sir William and Lady Allingham upon the morrow. This immediately required that all efforts be directed to the pressing of the best gowns they had brought with them.

St. Clare, who would naturally be present at any party given by the parents of his affianced bride, called for them the next evening in a stately berline that had belonged to his mother. "You are on time," he declared as he entered the hall to find all three ladies assembled there.

Ari's teasing rejoinder died on her lips. He seemed not at all the young man with whom she had squabbled and fought and laughed. Now he was a gentleman of fashion, a leader of society, elegant in black, a sapphire gleaming in the intricate folds of his neckcloth. She felt shy, awed, and very aware of him.

His gaze rested on her for a moment; was that admiration she read in his eyes? But why should it be?

He was probably just startled she was able to look other than a complete hoyden. And she must admit, she had her mother's determined efforts to thank for creating in her at least the semblance of a young lady.

In his well-sprung vehicle, they traveled the short distance in state, much to Diana's delight, and arrived in good time at Allingham Park. Few lights illumined the outside of the residence, which appeared to be about the size and age of the dower house. Candles blazed from every window though, casting a welcoming glow over the gravel drive. The coachman pulled up before the door, and St. Clare sprang down, then turned to assist first Mrs. Whitcombe, then Diana, from the carriage. Last, he reached a hand up to Ari, taking hers in a firm clasp.

The contact sent a shiver of nerves through her. She looked down, not meeting his gaze. He had no interest in her, she reminded herself. And she could have none in him. She was being foolish beyond permission. Almost at once he dropped her hand and turned to Mrs. Whitcombe, escorting that lady up the shallow steps.

The door opened as they reached it to reveal a man of advancing years, his portly figure covered in black and silver livery. He beamed on the viscount with a possessive eye. "Welcome, my lord," he said, and led them to a salon decorated in ivory and gold just off the main hall.

They entered to find the room inhabited by five other people. Ari was surprised to see Mr. Billingsworth, though she was not certain whether to be nervous at being under his scrutiny in company, or relieved that he might at last observe her at her best. Here, at least, she wasn't likely to disgrace herself. With him sat an elderly gentleman, also a clergyman. His rector, she guessed. She glanced at the others and saw Miss Allingham directing a shy smile toward her.

Sir William heaved himself to his feet and came forward to meet them. A gaunt woman in a gown of puce silk, presumably Lady Allingham, remained in her chair beside the hearth and regarded them through cool, unsmiling eyes down the length of her aristocratic nose. Ari made a shrewd guess they did not owe this invitation to their hostess. Sir William acknowledged the introductions with the same stiff manner he had shown to her the day before—a high stickler, Ari guessed. How could these two have produced anyone as sweet as their daughter?

Conversation, despite the best efforts of Mr. Billingsworth and Mrs. Whitcombe, did not flourish. The rector, who was introduced as Mr. Covington, placed himself at the side of Lady Allingham. That lady, beyond making stiffly polite comments to Mrs. Whitcombe, seemed to prefer to ignore the existence of the other women. To her patent annoyance, Diana talked gaily to St. Clare, who appeared to derive more enjoyment from her lively company than from the ponderous conversation of his host.

"Pray, call me Libby," whispered Miss Allingham as she drew Ari down to join her. "No one ever does, now that Charlie is dead. He was St. Clare's brother, you must know. You cannot imagine how I have longed for someone with whom I could be informal."

"Libby, then. And everyone calls me Ari."

"A lovely name," pronounced Mr. Billingsworth, taking the seat across from her.

Libby turned to him at once. "How is poor Mrs. Ottley? I was not able to visit her today, though I wished to very much."

Mr. Billingsworth's expression softened as he smiled at her. "She is feeling a trifle better, and so very grateful for the soup you brought her. Mrs. Ottley," he added, turning to Ari, "is growing quite old, I fear, and when she fell last week, she injured herself badly. She lives on a small farm near the village, though she might have to give it up soon."

Libby made an exclamation of regret. "She told me her papa ran the farm, and his before him."

Mr. Billingsworth inclined his head. "It would be a sad thing, indeed, but her own son is gone, and her grandson pressed into the navy. She has no one to help her."

"You must organize the other farmers to help her bring in her harvest," Libby declared.

Mr. Billingsworth's smile widened. "Such a kind heart. I have already done so, and asked the rectory housekeeper to pack up some comfrey and sage."

"And do not forget thyme," urged Libby, "for poor Mrs. Ottley tends to cough so dreadfully."

Ari sat back in her chair, forgotten, as the discussion roamed over the difficulties brought on a village with the approach of winter. They were soon on to the ingredients for the most nourishing broth, then which herbs any good housewife should have on hand for curing colds and influenza and chilblains. How perfect a couple these two would make, Ari reflected, watching the animation in both faces. So well matched as to temperament and interest.

But so very separated by fortune. Libby might make the most excellent clergyman's wife, but her father, despite his considerable wealth, had no living to offer an impoverished curate. And try as she might, she could not envision Libby's mother exchanging a viscount for a minor clergyman. For that matter, she doubted Libby would be willing to make that change either. How could any female not be attracted to a gentleman of St. Clare's stamp?

"Ari?" Diana's laughing voice broke across her thoughts. "St. Clare insists that Hannibal is perfectly trained, which is not at all what you have told me."

"Is it not?" demanded St. Clare, his eyes gleaming. "That is only because your sister, Miss Diana, has no concept of how to handle dogs."

Ari swelled with indignation. "Have I not? But

then, you must remember, Diana, that this is being said to you by someone who believes it the most acceptable thing in the world for great vicious brutes to maul poor innocent little kittens. So you see how little his opinion must matter."

"He has not hurt that kitten yet, has he?" St. Clare demanded. "And if you are so concerned about it, I do not understand why you do not keep it safe within doors."

She looked down her nose at him but knew the effect fell sadly short of its desired mark. "You obviously have little experience with animals, my lord, or you would know there can be no confining a cat once it has made up its mind to go outside. It cannot, like a dog, be trained to know better. Which the dog would if his master taught him correctly."

The spark of enjoyment burned bright in St. Clare's eyes. They both delighted in their argument. In fact, she very much enjoyed his liveliness of mind, his wicked sense of the ridiculous, his carefree, laughing eyes. Her own smile faded as she cast a sideways glance to where Libby and Mr. Billingsworth remained deep in serious conversation. She had no right to prefer another lady's fiancé.

No right, indeed. But every desire.

# Five

Ari awoke during the night to the pounding of rain against her window and howling wind rattling the pane. Then claws found her shoulder, and the kitten nestled against her cheek, curling up on her pillow. Its tail hair tickled her nose. Ari turned over, allowing Sappho the lion's share of the bedding, and drifted back to sleep.

She didn't awaken again until the pale, watery sunlight seeped through the draperies and fell across her face. She yawned, stretched, and reached out a hand to stroke the soft fur. Sappho wasn't there. She sat up and looked around but saw no traces of the kitten on her bed. Nor was the little thing in the basket Ari had set for it. She tucked her feet into her slippers and looked under the bed, but no eyes stared back at her from the dark depths. Curious, for the kitten rarely left the comforts of the blankets, Ari poked about the chamber, checking each of the kitten's known haunts. And then she reached the door and saw that it stood slightly ajar.

The faulty latch, she realized. This was not the first time her door had popped open. Sappho had probably taken advantage of this to go in search of an early breakfast. Ari threw on a morning gown, exchanged her slippers for more durable shoes, and headed off in search of her pet.

She called it as she descended the stairs, but no patter of tiny feet answered the summons. The lure of fresh cream, Ari reflected, and headed for the kitchen. As she entered the apartment, she found Rawlins at the back door, on her hands and knees with a cloth and bucket of soapy water.

The woman looked up. "The dratted thing was wide open," she said in disgust. "If you could have a word with his lordship's estate agent and get it fixed, I'd be very grateful, miss. There was mud everywhere."

"I can see. Yes, certainly, we must get it fixed. And it's not the only door that needs work." But it just might be the most important one, she realized with a sense of dismay. Rawlins had cleared away most of the mud washed in by the storm, but traces remained, tiny paw prints leading toward the exit. Sappho, it seemed, had gone out.

She returned to her room, donned her heavy cloak, then retraced her steps to the kitchen and exited the house. But in the yard, the featherweight kitten did not seem to have left even the tiniest of impressions in the damp earth. Ari stooped low, searching, knowing Sappho must have passed this way. Yet she hadn't left a trace.

Frustrated, she called, but no answer came. She hadn't really expected one, she supposed. But she had hoped. She tried the kitten's favorite stall in the stable but discovered no evidence the kitten had visited—no muddy print, no tiny nose peeping out from beneath the straw. Perplexed, and beginning to be a little worried, she went back into the yard. Sappho must be somewhere. But she had no idea at what time the kitten set forth on its illicit ramblings. By now it could be anywhere. Not willing to give up, she set forth along one of the paths, calling as she went.

From somewhere not far away, she could hear hoofbeats growing steadily closer. She must be near the Grange's drive, for she had headed in the opposite direction from the lane. The next moment something large crashed through the underbrush, and Hannibal bounded toward her, liberally splattered with mud. He thudded against her, smearing her skirts as his tongue lolled to one side and he panted happily.

"Hannibal!" St. Clare's shout carried easily on the chill air. "Come here, sir."

"He is busy covering me in mud at the moment," Ari called back. And why did her heart have to lift just at the sound of his voice? Or even at the sight of this deplorable hound, for that meant the master was near?

The hoofbeats stopped, then came the crunch of boots landing on gravel as St. Clare dismounted. He thrust his way through the brush, and there he was, tall, elegant in his deep blue riding coat, buckskins, and top boots, a muscle twitching at the corner of his mouth as if he fought back a smile at what he surveyed.

She looked down quickly, struggling against an overwhelming desire to become lost in his laughing brown eyes. This wouldn't do at all; she couldn't let herself be so beguiled, couldn't let herself crave what lay forever beyond her reach. She took refuge behind her usual caustic manner but found little solace in it. "Your help would be appreciated."

"He's only being friendly," St. Clare pointed out. He remained where he stood, the corners of his eyes crinkled with amusement.

It had been a mistake to allow her gaze to flicker back to him. She concentrated very hard on Hannibal. "How does that lessen the damage he does?"

Still with that intriguing muscle tugging at his mouth, he strode forward, grasped the errant dog by the scruff of the neck, and hauled him back. "The dratted beast has ruined your gown," he declared in surprisingly contrite tones. He surveyed her from the top of her smoothed-back hair to the toes of her mud-splattered shoes, and a frown creased his brow. "Whatever brought you out on such a morning?"

She willed her cheeks not to flush under his scrutiny, but to no avail. "Sappho," she admitted, then added quickly, "one cannot train a kitten, for they will wander."

St. Clare regarded her for a moment, a wicked gleam lighting his eye. He turned to Hannibal. "Sit, sir. We have a job for you. You will find Sappho for Miss Whitcombe. Is that understood? Find Sappho."

"Pray, do not be absurd! Those gigantic paws of his will destroy any traces the kitten might have left. And he will only frighten the poor little thing so it will never come out from wherever it must be hiding." She glared at St. Clare, aware he merely teased her, aware she wanted him to keep on doing so, aware she must not enjoy their verbal battles so much. With an effort, she turned away. "I shall simply have to wait for Sappho to come home on her own."

She started back the way she had come, only to slip on the muddy debris covering the path. St. Clare caught her elbow to steady her, then suggested she allow him to help her to the gravel drive, where she could walk with relative ease on an unshifting surface. She declined his aid but accompanied him to where he had left his horse with its reins hooked over a low branch. He freed it, then fell into step at her side, leading his mount.

"There is no need to escort me," she informed him as Hannibal panted happily between them. "I cannot lose my way, and no perils lurk—"

The hound pricked his ears, his nose snuffled, and the next moment he darted back into the underbrush. Ari and St. Clare exchanged a glance, then she hurried after the dog, thrusting branches aside to make a path.

She caught up to him burrowing energetically under a bush.

"Hannibal," St. Clare called, then added as he surveyed his pet, "if you think anything will spare you from the scrubbing tub after this, you are very much mistaken, sir."

Hannibal backed out slowly, something small and furry clasped gently in his mouth. Ari reached out a tentative hand, not wanting to alarm the dog into biting down, but he merely carried the unprotesting kitten to the base of a tree, where he proceeded to lie down in the mud, set the kitten on his front paws, and subject it to a thorough licking.

"There." The viscount watched his pet with a mixture of disapproval and amusement. "I told you he has his uses. I wouldn't be surprised if your kitten had come in search of him in the first place."

Ari cast him a darkling look.

"It is a great pity he cannot clean your gown as well," St. Clare added.

"Or your boots," she agreed.

The viscount looked down at them and swore. "My man will have a few things to say about these." He met her gaze, and a boyish grin spread over his face.

She found herself answering it, found herself sinking in an awareness of him that swept all else away. His power, his good humor, his laughing eyes . . . Despite the overcast sky and the persistent drizzle, warmth flooded through her as he continued to smile. Something more touched his expression, something in the depths of his eyes, something arrested, puzzled, almost troubled. She experienced an overwhelming urge to tell him everything was all right, to wipe the growing frown from his face.

Instead, she detached Sappho from the dog, told St. Clare again there was no need to accompany her, waved a falsely cheery hand over her shoulder, and hurried away. He was irritating and devastatingly masculine and engaged to someone else. It was of all things the most ludicrous that she should develop a tendre for him. A very foolish tendre. Quite ridiculous. It was only her reprehensible nature, rebelling because she had been told she must marry the curate. And Mr. Billingsworth was a very good man, kind and gentle and intelligent, giving every question due consideration and responding like a sensible gentleman. She was far from worthy of him. And St. Clare—

St. Clare was everything of which her dreams were made.

He thought in the same way she did. Her very happiness seemed to depend upon seeing him, upon watching his eyes light with amusement at a shared joke, upon making some comment and knowing he would understand without her having to explain. Upon just walking at his side in silence, because words were not necessary between them.

She hugged the kitten close, smearing mud over her bodice. She could not indulge in this foolishness. He was engaged to Libby, so there was no point in thinking about him. And she—

She would work very hard on becoming a proper wife for a vicar.

She spent the afternoon cleaning and mending her damaged gown, which drew shocked comments from her mother and teasing ones from Diana. It took far longer than the chore ought, simply because her heart and mind kept wandering into forbidden territory. Once, she found she had sewn a stretch of the torn flounce to the gown she currently wore, and had to snip the thread with care, then undo her laborious stitches until she could tie a knot.

Just when she was screaming internally for a diversion—*any* diversion—a visitor arrived. Mr. Billingsworth entered the room before she could set her work aside.

He regarded her for a moment, a slow smile of what

could only be relief crossing his somber features. "I am glad to see you find enjoyment in so commonplace a task. I would have thought it rather dull for your lively spirits. It is an excellent occupation for such inclement weather, is it not?"

She refrained from admitting she would much rather be tramping across the woods, possibly following a dog, possibly in the company of St. Clare— She broke off that thought and merely murmured a polite nothing.

"Pray, keep to your labors," he said as she stuffed the gown into her workbasket. "I have no desire to disturb you." With that he accepted Mrs. Whitcombe's offer of a cup of tea, stayed for the correct half hour, then took his leave, saying he had parish duties.

Mrs. Whitcombe sighed as the door closed behind him. "He has such excellent manners. I am truly grateful to my sister for arranging such a match." She cast an anxious glance toward Ari.

"It was very kind of her, indeed," agreed Ari, though a touch dutifully. "He is truly a most excellent gentleman. I—I hold him in the highest esteem."

And was that so very far from love? she wondered. Yes, a little voice cried within her, but she closed her mind to it. She must always admire Mr. Billingsworth for his kindness and principles, and that was far more than many young ladies could boast upon entering the married state. She was very lucky. And that reflection only lowered her spirits even more. She set another stitch, wondering if she would ever learn to accept the pastime without loathing.

A footstep sounded beyond the door, and it opened to reveal Rawlins, an unaccustomed flush to her cheeks and a spark of indignation lighting her fine gray eyes. "If you please, miss," she said to Ari, "there is a great, lumbering, muddy dog pawing at the back door, and try as I might, I cannot get it to go away."

Hannibal! Ari's heart leapt. Had St. Clare come for some reason— She threw her needlework aside and hurried to the kitchen.

Sappho crouched on her side of the door, pawing at it. Ari could hear the scratching from without. She picked up the kitten and set it on a chair, then opened the door a crack. Hannibal thrust his way into the kitchen, knocking her aside. He bounded to where Sappho peered over the edge of the seat. The massive jaws closed over the kitten, then the dog, with Sappho clasped in its mouth, bounded back outside.

Ari set off after it, calling for it to stop, to return at once, but the insufferable hound paid her no heed. It leapt on through the mud, its ridiculous tail wagging as it disappeared beyond the stable.

# Six

Ari ran across the yard in pursuit, turning onto the path she had followed only that morning. She was probably ruining another gown and thereby condemning herself to another day's mending. Vexed, she pushed on, following the racket of the exuberant hound's passage. Then another sound reached her, St. Clare's deep, ringing voice calling the wretched animal. She slowed, and her heart turned over painfully in her chest.

Hannibal, however, kept going, plunging through the underbrush in the viscount's general direction. Ari followed as best she could, for she chose to go around the shrubs rather than through them.

"What the devil have you there, sir?" St. Clare demanded from much closer at hand. A moment of silence followed, then he burst out laughing. "Bad dog. No, sir. Put it down this instant!" But the amusement in his voice destroyed the force of his words.

Ari pushed her way through a stand of saplings, and he looked up, right at her. She must look a dreadful mess, she realized, for she had not dressed for the outdoors. Her hair—

"You have reason to be angry, I fear," he said. "Though it isn't in the least bit injured. It seems to be enjoying itself."

"How anyone could enjoy being grasped by that great, drooling mouth!" Ari stepped forward carefully, her slipper sliding in a muddy patch.

St. Clare reached out, catching her arm, and her awareness focused on that single point of contact. With an effort, she dragged her mind from it. "Revolting beast," she declared, her voice a trifle shaky.

The viscount released her and went to work removing the kitten from the dog's gentle jaws. When at last he had it free, he regarded Sappho with misgivings. "It is rather wet, I fear." He pulled out a handkerchief and dried the kitten as best he could. Holding it at arm's length, he eyed it critically. It mewed and struggled. "There, good as new," he pronounced, and handed it to her.

For several moments she was occupied by the task of settling it in her arm while keeping its claws from attaching themselves to her. She looked up to find him watching her with that barely suppressed laughter in his eyes, and his amusement poured through her like liquid fire. He was betrothed to Libby, she reminded herself. And even if he were not, she knew herself to be a dreadful hoyden, and no more suitable a wife for a viscount than for a vicar.

The next morning, Ari stood at the window of the back salon, staring out into the cool, crisp morning air. Behind her, Diana worked through a series of scales on the pianoforte, her touch light and flying. Ari could see no need to play watchdog. Diana adored her music. She would probably keep at it the entire day.

From above stairs, she could hear her mother and Rawlins moving about, checking linens. It was beginning to seem as if they would remain the entire winter, for Mr. Billingsworth showed no signs of offering for her. Not that she could blame him. It must take a great deal to screw oneself up to the sticking point. And there she went, using vulgar expressions again, even if only to herself. It was no wonder he doubted her suitability to be his wife. And if it weren't for her mother and Diana, she would tell her aunt not to bribe the poor man so.

A deep sigh escaped her. It was far too beautiful a day to remain indoors. St. Clare must be outside, probably with a gun and with Hannibal racing about, startling all the birds. If only their path would lead up the drive, past her window—

But this was being foolish beyond permission. If St. Clare hadn't already offered for Libby, she might make the attempt to convince him she was just the wife for him. Not that he would be likely to believe it. He needed a lady every bit as respectable and proper as did a vicar.

The knocker on the door sounded, surprising her. She couldn't see the front of the house, nor the approach. Diana broke off and started to rise, her expression vexed, as if she deplored this interruption.

"Keep practicing," Ari told her, and hurried into the hall. Rawlins would be busy upstairs; she'd answer the door herself.

A minute later she opened it to find Mr. Billingsworth standing on the upper step, his expression somber. "What a pleasant surprise," she declared, standing back to allow him to enter. "Diana is in the salon, if you would care to join her while I run upstairs to tell my mother you have come."

"Pray, do not bother." He hesitated a moment, then plunged on. "It is you I have come to see."

Ari's fingers twisted in her muslin skirts, and her heart sank. This was it. There could be no more hope of escape, no more daydreaming of a very different future. She forced a smile and showed him into the cozy library. A sudden chill crept through her, one no fire could remedy. Which was just as well, she realized the next moment, for none had been kindled in the empty grate. She perched on the edge of a straight-backed chair and gestured him toward the elegant sofa opposite.

Instead, he paced to the hearth, then turned to face her, the gaze of his grave eyes resting on her face. "I have received a letter from your aunt this day," he began, then broke off. A rueful smile tugged at the corner of his mouth. "That is hardly the way to begin what I have to say."

"No, it is exactly the way." Ari met his gaze squarely. "She is pressing you to offer for me, is she not?"

Mr. Billingsworth hesitated. "It is the wish of her heart to see us both settled," he said with admirable diplomacy.

It was the wish of her heart to meddle, Ari reflected fiercely, but knew she must be grateful. She straightened. "If you have any reservations about my suitability— No, pray do not interrupt me. It is best if we speak plainly to each other."

He considered a moment, then nodded gravely.

"I know I am far too lively," she rushed on.

"Lively, it is true," he said judiciously. "And full of laughter and wit. But I have also never known you to speak an unkind word. You possess a generosity of spirit that will endear you to my parishioners. As it has endeared you to me," he added with the air of one remembering a rehearsed speech.

She studied his face intently but could detect no signs of uncertainty. He had, it seemed, accepted the inevitable. And now so must she. She drew a deep breath. "I am fully aware of the honor you do me, Mr. Billingsworth. I promise you, I shall do my very best to assure you never regret your own generosity of spirit." She rose.

He took her hand. "I shall write to your aunt this evening."

And probably to his mother and his brother as well,

to set their minds at rest that their future was secured. As was hers, and her family's.

He raised her fingers to his lips. "We shall be quite content together," he reassured her. "I will do my utmost to make certain that we are."

The door swung open and Diana and Libby stood on the threshold. Diana's avid gaze took in the scene before her, and her eyes widened in a mixture of relief and amusement.

Libby, just behind her, drew back. "I am so sorry—"

"I was just taking my departure," said Mr. Billingsworth, displaying all the signs of a gentleman undergoing acute embarrassment. "Miss Whitcombe? Shall I speak to your mother?"

"No, there is not the least need." Color burned in her cheeks, as if they had been caught in some reprehensible conduct.

He bowed to her and exited the room. But as he passed Libby, he looked into the girl's face, then quickly away. "Miss Allingham," he said softly, then was gone.

"Has he offered for you?" cried Diana as soon as the soft shutting of the front door assured his departure. "Oh, pray, do not keep me in suspense! Are you to marry him? Are we to have a home?"

Libby remained in the doorway, her expression solemn. Ari looked away from so much seriousness. "He will probably read the banns this Sunday," she said, and could only hope her listeners could not detect the hollowness of her heart.

"Oh, I must tell Mama at once!" Diana cried, and darted from the room.

Libby took a step inside. "I—I wish you every happiness, my dear Ari. Indeed, it must be yours, for I do not know a kinder gentleman than Mr. Billingsworth."

Ari sighed. "No, he certainly deserves better than myself."

"You will make an excellent vicar's wife," Libby declared with a touch more determination than conviction.

Ari grimaced. "I have my doubts. And I fear poor Mr. Billingsworth has them as well. But I will try my best not to let him regret this morning's work."

Libby stared at her. "To—to be sure."

Ari pulled herself together. "How pleasant that you have come to call. Do sit down and have some tea."

Libby shook her head. "I—I cannot stay."

Her eyes had misted over, Ari realized. The girl turned blindly toward the door, only to halt as Diana hurried in, hauling their mama by the hand.

"Oh, my love," cried Mrs. Whitcombe. "Is it indeed true? Oh, the dear, blessed man, to take us on. You do like him, do you not, Ari? You are bound to deal comfortably with each other, you know. It cannot be otherwise, for he is so very good." She turned to Libby. "This is the greatest happiness for me, for you must know I was at my wit's end worrying over how to provide for my girls, until my dear sister arranged this match. And I must say, I am quite relieved to discover Mr. Billingsworth is such a very good sort of man. I was in the greatest dread Ari might not like him, or that he might not be able to bring himself to overlook the impetuosity in her nature. But with his own mama and brother to provide for—" She broke off, as if she realized she was being indiscreet. "But all is to be delightfully arranged."

After murmured congratulations, Libby repeated her excuses and departed. Ari crossed to the window and watched the girl's hurried retreat down the path. The news of the impending marriage had distressed her. Why should it—unless she cared for Mr. Billingsworth herself? But Libby was engaged to St. Clare, and as kind as the curate might be, there could be no comparison between the two men.

Driven to the point of distraction by her mother's

effusive delight, Ari slipped out of the house and set forth for a long ramble through the woods. More than an hour passed before she began to pay attention to her surroundings, and she found herself near a wide stream she hadn't seen before. She presumed herself still to be on Grange lands, for she hadn't noticed any boundary markers. She changed course to follow the path that wound along the water's edge.

Perhaps twenty minutes later she heard a deep, familiar bark. The next minute Hannibal appeared over the top of a rise. His ears pricked and he sped across the grassy space toward her. Ari braced herself for the inevitable impact.

"Hannibal!" St. Clare's sharp voice stopped the hound in mid-stride. "Hannibal, where the devil—" The viscount emerged from a line of trees and stopped, staring across at her. "Get over here!" he snapped at Hannibal, who slunk back to his side.

Here was someone else in a mood as strange and irritated as her own, Ari reflected. On the whole, she wished she might avoid this meeting.

But he walked toward her, stopping several paces away. "Did Miss Allingham come to speak with you today?" he demanded.

"Only briefly."

"Then, it is settled?" His words came out clipped, as if he found no pleasure in speaking them.

"What is?" She had no desire to discuss her engagement with anyone—especially him.

"That you will support her through the wedding, of course," he snapped. "I thought you females would talk of nothing else."

His wedding. Why must it hurt so much for him to mention it? Her chin thrust out. "I am afraid that my own news must have overshadowed it. You see, I am to be married also."

St. Clare's brow lowered. "So you managed to bring

poor Billingsworth up to scratch, did you? I suppose he didn't have the bottom to defy your aunt."

Ari stiffened. "If you mean to imply he has been forced to offer for me—"

"Of course he has." St. Clare glared at her. "Good God, you cannot think yourself suitable to the role of a vicar's wife, can you? A sad dance you will lead him. I can only hope you do not both live to regret it!"

That he echoed her own secret fears did little to improve her flaring temper. Her hands clenching at her sides, she glared back at him. "I shall do everything in my power to see he never does regret it, for I cannot imagine a better husband. I can only be grateful I shall never have to put up with a foul-tempered, autocratic, pigheaded pleasure-seeker!"

His eyes narrowed. "And I," he said through gritted teeth, "must be grateful never to be tied to a shrew-tongued vixen!" And with that he turned on his heel, called savagely for Hannibal, and stomped off.

Ari stared after him, shaken by the force of his anger, at how much his words hurt. It had been her fault, of course, all her fault. She should never have spoken as she had. If only she could run far away, escape his anger. At least she would marry in a very short time, and then she could escape this estate, escape St. Clare forever.

Tears stung her eyes, but she fought them back, refusing to give in to them as she made her way back to the dower house.

# Seven

Ari passed a restless night and arose late, still tired and depressed. She donned a gown at random, twisted her hair in a knot, then made her way down to the breakfast parlor. Only her mother sat within, sipping tea and eating buttered rolls. A crumb-filled plate showed that Diana had already departed. Ari selected a bun but found she had no appetite.

"My love, you are dreadfully pale this morning." Her mother set down her cup and peered at her. "Do you think you are sickening for something? Shall I call Rawlins? You may count upon it, she will know what to do. Never have I known anyone more capable of finding just the right remedy for whatever ails one. How well I recall—"

"I am perfectly well, Mama," Ari said, breaking across Mrs. Whitcombe's outpourings. "It is only the headache, and I shall take a walk to clear away the cobwebs." She rose and made good her escape.

She set forth a short time later, wrapped in her pelisse, with no specific goal in mind. She would stay clear of the estate, of course; she didn't want to run the risk of encountering St. Clare again. Her irresolute steps followed the lane toward the village, then on impulse she turned down a path bordered by a yew hedge that led toward the Allingham estate.

She had not gone very far when she heard Libby, from the other side of the shrubbery, exclaim, "I know you will be happy. You must be happy. Ari Whitcombe is so very intelligent and clever, your new parish must surely admire her."

"It is a curse to be poor!" declared Mr. Billingsworth in a vibrant, quavering voice.

Ari moved ahead a step to a gap between the bushes. The two stood a scant twenty yards away, facing each other across a distance of six feet, staring intently at each other. Ari was about to announce her presence, but Libby's next words kept her silent.

"I—I would live in a hovel with you," came the girl's trembling response.

An exclamation escaped the curate. "This does us no good. If we had only declared ourselves to each other before— But to what purpose? I have always known your papa would never consider me an eligible suitor. What have I that could compare to the title and holdings of St. Clare?"

"Worth of character!" cried Libby.

"St. Clare is an excellent landlord and a gentleman in every respect." His tone held mild reproof. "And do not forget," he added, his voice gentling, "you will have a position to be envied in Society."

"But I do not want to go into Society!" Libby wailed. "Everyone is so conscious of their positions and their worth, and if you do not measure up to their standards, they treat you to the most devastating snubs."

"No one will snub a viscountess."

Libby blinked back tears. "If only my mama were not set upon this match! If only I had known that you returned my regard—"

The curate shook his head. "It would make no difference. And we were foolish beyond permission ever to have allowed the subject to come up between us now, of all times." He awarded her a short bow and turned away, then stopped as his gaze fell upon Ari. "Miss—Miss Whitcombe!"

"Oh!" gasped Libby. She covered her flaming cheeks with her hands.

Ari stepped onto the gravel path, which crunched beneath her booted foot. "It seems we are in quite a muddle," she said with forced cheerfulness.

"Oh!" wailed Libby again. "Ari, I do beg your pardon, only—" She broke off.

"Only there are times when one's heart will not be silenced?" Ari asked, forcing a smile. What was she doing? her conscience screamed. Or half her conscience. The other half drove her forward, caused her to throw her own considerations to the winds for the sake of these two.

Mr. Billingsworth cleared his throat. "I—" He stopped, then tried again. "It is possible you are suffering from a misunderstanding."

"I was," agreed Ari. "But not now. I believe everything is at last clear. You knew that Libby's parents would never countenance your suit, because you are only a curate with no prospects. My aunt, having no way of knowing your heart was engaged, proposed this match with me. And if you could not have your heart's desire, then at least you could provide for your mother and brother."

Mr. Billingsworth blanched. "When you put it in that manner, I seem the most despicable cad. I assure you, Miss Whitcombe, I would not have offered for you if I could not value you."

Her lips tugged into a rueful smile. "Thank you. Nor would I have accepted if I did not hold you in the highest esteem. But you must see, the situation has altered."

"It has not," Mr. Billingsworth insisted. "If you will do me the honor—"

"I will not." She drew a steadying breath. "Not now. No, please." She held up a hand to stem his flow of words. "We must set our minds to discover a means by which you two may wed."

"But it is impossible!" declared Libby. A tear trickled down her cheek. "I—I have always known it to be so."

"Her parents have harbored the greatest matrimonial ambitions for her," the curate explained.

"Then she must defy them," Ari decided.

Mr. Billingsworth shook his head. "You forget my own circumstances, I fear. Without the living offered by your aunt, my prospects do not bear thinking about."

"Then my aunt must give you that living." Ari considered for a moment. "I shall write to her this night and make it clear that I am shockingly unworthy of her kindness, and that it is through no fault of yours that her scheme has come to naught. Never fear, she will relent. She is a kindly soul."

"But if my mama guesses—" Libby's face paled.

Mr. Billingsworth grasped Libby's hand and pressed it.

"Obtain a special license," Ari suggested. "Once you are actually married, there will be nothing she can do."

Libby's chin quavered. "But she and my papa will be so very angry!"

"They may be as angry as they choose," Ari said. "You will not be here to endure it, and you may count on Mr. Billingsworth to protect you if they pay you a visit." It took some time to convince the pair that their happiness was well on the way to being assured, and that they had only to display a little resolution to carry the day. At last, Ari turned her steps back toward the dower house. What, she wondered, would she tell her mama and Diana? They would not take kindly to her casting away their security.

But what else could she do? She had rarely met two people so ideally suited to one another. The knowledge of how happy they would be must be a comfort to her. It might well be her only one. How angry everyone else would be with her.

Her aunt, especially, would have every right to be furious. Somehow, she must convince that lady that she, Ari, had acted for the best, or poor Mr. Billingsworth might still lose that living.

And St. Clare— She came to an abrupt halt. How angry would he be? She didn't know whether or not he loved Libby; she had sometimes wondered—hoped—he did not. But he had his share of pride, and it would not please him to be thrown over for a curate. No, he would be livid—with her. Would he evict them from the dower house? She had no clear idea what the terms of their agreement had been, whether they held the house for a specific length of time, or if he had simply allowed them to use it. She might well find herself without a roof over her head because of this day's work.

# Eight

The letter Ari wrote that afternoon was perhaps the most difficult she had to compose. It wasn't easy to blend the right proportion of apology, conviction she acted correctly, assertions of the couple's blamelessness, and her own guilt, all the while trying to omit any trace of the fear that clamored within her. While her mama and Diana busied themselves elsewhere, she slipped out of the house and walked to the village to post the missive. Her steps dragged, and only repeated assertions to herself that she behaved in the sole manner possible kept her going. She carried before her, like a lamp illuminating the darkness in her heart, the certainty of the couple's happiness.

It would take a day for the letter to reach her aunt, then another before any reply could possibly come back. Longer, perhaps, if her aunt took time to consider the situation. She might well refuse. But Ari could not let herself believe that. Nor could she deny that sharing her guilt and fear for the future was a strong sense of relief that she might not have to marry poor Mr. Billingsworth after all.

Well, until the answer appeared on her doorstep, she need not trouble either her mother or Diana with what she had done—with what she had cast away. Bad news always arrived too soon as it was. Let them have a few more days of peace.

During the long hours of the night that followed, she lay awake, cudgeling her brain for some—any—solution to their difficulties. Not surprisingly, none came. There was no solution. She had condemned her family, who had counted on her, to poverty. She could only be grateful her mother and sister were not yet plagued by worries, that for a little while longer she would be spared their recriminations.

The following morning dawned drizzly and dark, confining them all within doors. Diana, who trailed embroidery silk for Sappho to attack, looked up suddenly. "Mr. Billingsworth has not come to call on you, Ari."

Ari froze. She was not ready to explain—

Mrs. Whitcombe beamed. "He is a very conscientious young man, Diana. He will put the needs of his parish before his own desires. He would come if he could."

"Winter is fast approaching," said Ari quickly. "There must be any number of things he needs to accomplish in the village and the surrounding farms."

What, precisely, these might be, she had not the slightest idea. But Diana accepted her words and returned to her entertainment of Sappho. Nor did she mention the matter again, though the days crept past.

On the morning of the sixth, not Mr. Billingsworth but Libby Allingham arrived on their doorstep, breathless, becomingly pink, her eyes sparkling. "Oh, please, Ari," she gasped as soon as Rawlins admitted her to the salon where the ladies sat at their correspondence, "will you come for a walk with me?"

Mrs. Whitcombe sighed. "It will be the very thing, my love, for you have been fidgeting for days. We shall not expect you back until nuncheon."

Ari excused herself to change into her jean half boots and don her pelisse and bonnet. As soon as they set forth, Libby, who had taken her arm, squeezed it. "Oh, Ari, I cannot tell you how happy I am. Your aunt has written to Mr. Billingsworth, and he is to have the vicarage. Old Mr. Covington—you remember our rector—is waiting at the church to marry us this minute! Oh, do say you will stand up with me, dearest Ari? I owe all my happiness to you."

Ari responded with what enthusiasm she could muster and fought back the sinking sensation in the pit of her stomach. She had done it. Libby and Mr. Billingsworth would be together. And as for her own family—

Firmly, she slammed the door against such thoughts—for now, at least. She would not spoil this morning for her friends. Fortunately, she did not have to speak much. Libby beguiled the walk to the church with plans for the future, with the cleverness of her bridegroom in having obtained a special license from the bishop, and with her own deceit in smuggling her clothes from her home.

"And Mama will forgive me once she has grown accustomed to the idea," Libby went on. "She never did like St. Clare, you must know. She used to call him rackety, and say he had the most reprehensible streak of funning, and that only his title made him acceptable to her. And she has never had anything but praise for my dear Mr. Billingsworth."

Ari suspected Lady Allingham would shortly have a great deal other than praise for that gentleman, once news of this day's work reached her. In a choice between goodness of heart and a title, Lady Allingham would unhesitatingly choose the latter. That Libby did not spoke to her credit.

"How will you tell them?" she asked, curious.

Libby looked down. "I have arranged for a letter to be delivered to them late this afternoon, before they will have time to wonder at the length of my absence. By then, my dear Mr. Billingsworth and I will be wed and away. They will grow accustomed to it," she added with force, as if the determination of her words could make them come true.

They at last reached the church to find a dilapidated gig with two large portmanteaus and a valise strapped precariously to its back. A single horse stood in the harness, head down, one back ankle cocked, waiting with the patience of an animal that would rather wait than be off and doing. Libby, almost running now in her eagerness, drew Ari up the stone steps and into the building.

Three gentlemen, all members of the clergy, sat in the front pew, deep in serious conversation. As the ladies' footsteps echoed up the aisle, the men looked up, and Mr. Billingsworth sprang to his feet, hurrying to meet them. He grasped Libby's hands, and the smile on his face made Ari's heart ache with a longing to experience such a love. He led his bride forward, and Ari stood to one side while the other clergyman stood beside Mr. Billingsworth. Mr. Covington read the service, then suddenly it was over, Mr. Billingsworth was kissing Libby, then hurrying her down the aisle, eager to be away to their new home. Ari followed them outside and watched Libby's new husband hand her tenderly into the gig.

"Ari!" Libby suddenly cried as Mr. Billingsworth took his place at her side. "Dearest Ari, I must beg you to do me one more favor, though you have done so much for us already. Will you give this to St. Clare?" She drew a folded sheet of paper, sealed with a wafer, from her reticule. "And tell him I apologize most sincerely."

Ari took it, though with considerable reluctance, and clutched it as she stood waving good-bye to her last hope as the couple drove merrily away in the gig.

Mr. Covington sighed as the carriage rounded a bend, taking it out of sight. "I do not suppose this is the last any of us will hear about this," he said with a lurking amusement in his eyes. "Still, I cannot regret it."

"No," said Ari. "Nor can I."

But now she must face the consequences of her actions. She must face her mama and tell her she had thrown away her one chance. And then she must face St. Clare. She turned to trudge back to the dower house, sunk in gloom.

The sound of hissing and spitting, followed by an excited bark, broke across her reverie as she neared the small stable. And there was Hannibal pressed against the stable door, with poor Sappho pinned under one massive paw. With a vexed exclamation, Ari strode forward and grasped the giant hound about the neck, yelling at it, trying to drag it off but unable to move the giant creature.

"Let me." St. Clare's voice sounded behind her.

The struggle had occupied her utterly; she hadn't heard him approach. She stepped aside, trembling all over, as the viscount grasped his faithful companion by the scruff of the neck. "Stop!" he commanded, and the hound went limp, sprawling on the ground and panting with a perfectly demented look on his face.

"Is that ridiculous kitten all right?" he demanded in exasperated tones.

On top of the stress, the worry she had endured over the last several days, this proved too much for her. She rounded on him, shaking with tangled emotions. "I doubt you would care in the least!" she cried. "You consider nothing but your own will and desires."

He blinked at her, apparently taken aback by her tirade.

She forged ahead, unable to stop the disastrous flow of words. "Could you not see how unhappy Libby has been?"

"If she is unhappy," he pointed out in the tones of one reasoning with a Bedlamite, "she has only to tell me. We have known each other since she was in her cradle."

"Yes, and her mama has planned your marriage for that long as well," Ari shot back. "What say could poor Libby possibly have against her mama's ambition?"

He frowned. "Libby has never so much as hinted she did not like the idea of marriage to me. She's a good, quiet girl with common sense, not a shred of a romantic notion in her head."

"Which only goes to show how little you truly know her!"

"Has she a romantic notion?" St. Clare demanded.

"Could you never tell?"

He took a moment to work that out. "Do you mean to tell me she's in love with someone else and has accepted me only because her parents won't countenance her choice?"

The patent chagrin on his face caused Ari to regret her outburst. She should have controlled her shattered emotions, broken the news to him in a kinder manner. And as for Libby— How could the foolish girl *not* love St. Clare? How could anyone not? True, he was proud, he could even be arrogant, but that was all part of what made him so—so very much himself.

"I'll talk to her," he decided. "I'll not have her forced—"

"There is no need." Ari drew Libby's letter from her reticule. "She asked me to give you this." She walked away, carrying the kitten into the stable, and perched on the step of the old farm cart that stood within. She could only hope Libby had phrased her missive gently.

Several minutes passed, then booted footsteps approached. She looked up quickly; she hadn't expected him to come in, but to leave, to seek solitude to lick his raw wound. "I am so very sorry," she said softly. "Do you mind dreadfully?"

He shook his head, his expression mournful. "The blow to my consequence. I doubt I shall ever recover. For my intended bride to prefer a curate to a viscount—" He shook his head once more. "Lord, the poor, silly chit. If only she had told me!"

"There was nothing she could tell. She and Mr. Billingsworth never declared themselves to each other because both thought it hopeless."

"So no one knew—even them." He rubbed his chin. "Your aunt has persuaded my cousin Gregory to bestow the living upon Mr. Billingsworth anyway—at your request." His gaze settled on her face. "You have sacrificed much for that hapless couple."

She shook her head. "I could hardly have married him when he loved another."

He continued to study her. "And your heart was not involved?"

"Not in the least."

"What will you do now?"

She drew a deep breath, and it escaped in a quavering sigh. "I don't know. I—I am not in the least looking forward to telling Mama I have thrown away our one chance for security."

"No," he agreed. "I doubt she will be pleased."

She cast him a darkling look. "If it were only myself, I could go as a governess. But that does not provide a home for Mama or Diana. Perhaps my aunt will take them in, though she is more likely to cast us off utterly for my refusal to fall in with her plans."

"There is another option," he suggested with a touch of diffidence.

She looked up, curious, afraid to hope.

"You were willing to accept one marriage of convenience. Might you consider another?"

The surge of longing amazed her, a heart hunger that snatched her breath away. Yet what if he meant someone else—

"I realize men of the cloth seem to be more desirable as marriage partners than noblemen are, but do you think you could sink so low as to become a viscountess?"

Only if you love me—the thought raced through her mind. She could know no greater happiness. But if he did not, if he offered for her out of friendship and pity— She didn't know if she could bear his altruistic kindness when she longed for so much more.

"Ari." There was a gentle command in his voice. "Look at me."

She did, her troubled gaze searching his face.

A slight smile tugged at his mouth, only to slip awry. "I want you for my wife. I've known it ever since I first laid eyes on you waving that broom at poor Hannibal. But there was nothing I could do about it—then. Now—" He broke off, then continued. "All I ask is that you give me the chance to win your love."

She stared at him, her heart too full to speak.

"If not for my sake," he went on, "or your sister's, or your mother's, then for theirs." He gestured toward the ground. "You cannot wish to part them."

She lowered her gaze to where Hannibal lay at St. Clare's feet, Sappho between his front paws while he industriously licked the small head.

"No." She studied the furry pair. "It would be cruel." Then she added in a rush, the words spilling out of her, "But it would tear my heart apart even more to be parted from you."

Complete silence greeted her declaration. Then, "My dearest love" broke from him in husky tones. He grasped her hand and drew her from her seat and into his arms.

She experienced a moment of stunned awe to find herself pressed against that strong chest, his hand twining in her hair. Then his mouth pressed against hers with an ardor that took her breath away and sent her senses reeling. She melted against him, lost in a radiant glow, assured that her love was amply returned.

And at their feet, Hannibal panted happily as Sappho batted at his paws.

# Cat's Cradle

Shannon Donnelly

# One

"Bea, you shameless hussy, where have you gotten to?"

Emaline Adair Pearson held the lantern higher to stare into the gloom, and her hand trembled slightly from nerves strung too tight. She should not be here. And the dark, empty rooms seemed to mock her errand and rebuke her presence.

She had no place here any longer. No claim.

But she had to fetch Bea home.

*Oh, drat Bea. And drat this gloomy September day. And drat Newell too.*

The lantern's light reached a timid glow around her, slipping over a huge scarred, oak table. The yellow pool of light just reached up the nearest wall to expose half-emptied shelves and dusty, rat-nibbled, leather-bound books too ponderous to interest anyone.

Newell had certainly stripped the house of anything he could carry or have carried out, she thought, glancing at the single enormous mahogany, high-backed wing chair covered in green hide and left beside the empty hearth. That, and the table, were the last occupants of what had once been a well-furnished library.

Well, it served Newell right that he had lost the manor, for he had taken such bad care of the estate.

But, oh, she wished that she could kick him for endangering her home in the bargain.

And then her cheeks warmed at such uncharitable thoughts. John, if he looked down on her and the boys from heaven now, would not be pleased.

A slamming of wood—no doubt a loose shutter buffeted in the autumn winds—startled her, making her jump.

Clutching her woolen cloak closer with her free hand, she gave a nervous glance around the deserted library—a room she had once loved. She should not have thought of ghosts, of John, gone now these five years. Such thoughts in an empty house on a dying autumn day did not make for good company.

Turning back to her errand, she peered into the darkness again. "Bea," she called, trying to hold rein on a temper made short by her desire to be gone.

Emaline had slipped in through a broken casement window that led to the shooting room—probably the same path Bea had used to enter. A pane had been missing from the window for three years, but it had been longer still since Newell had inherited the house and promptly left for London and the restless life he had always wanted.

She moved forward slowly. The floorboards creaked but did not break, and no sign of damp streaked the ceiling or stained the wood. However, she could not but feel as if she were walking through a graveyard.

A cemetery of memories.

She could recall a time when a fire danced warm in the large dark hole of a hearth, when books in Morocco red with gold lettering lined the shelves, all tidy and orderly. Aunt Mary would sit before the fire, next to Emaline's own mother, both stitching, while Uncle Walter read to them. Usually something improving, such as Milton.

Emaline had loved the deep rumble of her uncle's voice, but she had not been fond of the grim John Milton.

Newell had positively hated the poet's work.

But that had all been in a different time. A time before influenza carried off her mother and her aunt. A time before age had closed her uncle's eyes for the last time. A time before she had married, and before she and the boys had moved to take up tenancy at the gate house.

A time before that wretched Newell had lost Adair Manor.

*Oh, drat you, Newell. How could you lose the house!*

Regrets, however, were not a luxury she cared to indulge in, and so she put back her shoulders to stand a little taller. She really must find Bea and get home before the shortened day turned to night.

"Bea?" she called again, trying to make her voice coaxing. "Bea?"

And then from behind her an amused masculine voice nearly made her heart stop.

" 'To be or not to be?' Is that your question?"

She whirled, her cloak flying out around her and the lantern bobbling in her grip.

A dark figure leaned against the door frame, ominously large and daunting. For an instant, she feared she honestly had summoned a spirit. But as the lantern wobbled in her unsteady hand, the shadow strode forward, sweeping the metal handle from her grip. The light danced over her specter, giving him life.

He wore no hat, and his sun-warmed brown hair spilled loose and curled over the collar of his coat. He was tall. So tall that she had to lean back to stare up at him. An arrogant nose dominated a life-worn face, and she decided as she studied that face that he had to be one of Newell's friends. He had that look of dissipation about him and far too sensual a mouth for any woman's peace of mind.

He put the lantern down on the oak table and then said, humor still in his voice, "I would appreciate if you would not set fire to my house before I've had a chance to inspect it."

She had been frozen by his sudden appearance and by the mortification of being caught where she should not be, but now she straightened, outrage coursing through her.

"Your house?" Heat flamed up her neck and into her cheeks. So it was him. The gamester. She knew all about him from Newell's letter. She narrowed her eyes and did not bother to hide her disdain. "Of course. You must be Sir Ashten Ravenhill."

Sir Ashten's eyes widened. They were the color of an autumn forest, a mix of browns and greens in shifting patterns. Amusement danced in those colors just now, and it irked her that he found something in her words to smile at. She wasn't used to bandying words with harden gamesters, and she did not want to become accustomed to such a habit.

Oh, she could throttle Newell for forcing her into this position.

With a warm smile, Sir Ashten said, "I didn't know there was an 'of course' to my identity."

"My cousin wrote me of you," she told him. "And of how you gained Adair Manor from him. And I will have you know that he wrote me after I had sent him my six pound and five for next quarter, so you may apply to him if you wish the cost of my lease of the gate house."

His smile lifted into a grin as she spoke, and she wished now that temper had not led her into those hot words. How stupid. The man had just won a house—and no doubt all of whatever money Newell had had left to him. Six and five for a quarter's rent would not matter to him.

"I shall keep that in mind," he said, and then perched on the edge of the oak table, one leg swinging free and easy. He wore riding clothes and a gray greatcoat with three tiers of rain-spattered capes.

She glanced at his clothes, and envy crawled loose inside her. Oh, but they were lovely, made from fine cloth, cut to display his lean muscles and show off his male form. Self-conscious, she clutched her woolen cloak even closer over her twice-mended blue dress, which had the sheen of age upon it.

Still smiling, he said, "Before we get into the issue of rents, there's another matter I'd like to settle. You know of me, but who are you—besides Newell's cousin? And why are you housebreaking?"

Her gaze snapped back to his face. "I am not housebreaking."

"Someone invited you in, then?"

"No. That is. . . .well . . . I used to live here."

The colors danced in his eyes again, lightening them to almost pure green. He folded his arms. "So you invited yourself back inside?"

"I did not think anyone would be here," she said, half faltering over her poor excuse.

"Well, I can see how that would make it necessary, then, for you to break in."

She fought the urge to stamp her worn boot on the dusty floor for how aggravating he was being. "I did nothing. The window was already broken."

"And that makes all the difference. Well, you are quite the prettiest housebreaker I've met, but do not blush, sweets, for I've not met all that many housebreakers. You're my first, in fact."

He grinned again, and she clenched her hands to keep from giving him an unladylike box on his ears.

With her temper simmering, she glared at him. "I am not blushing. And I am not a housebreaker. And I—"

A piteous mewing interrupted, and she swung around, the provoking Sir Ashten forgotten at the sound of her cat in distress. "Bea," she said, hurrying toward the far wall.

Another mew led her to a giant oak press cupboard,

ornately carved with flowers and vines, and large enough to take up twelve feet of the wall opposite the windows. Kneeling, she swung open the half-ajar bottom door, calling out tentatively, "Bea?"

From his perch on the table, Ash watched his pretty housebreaker poke into some monstrosity of a cupboard. He had not quite decided if he was dealing with the village lunatic or with that even more dangerous creature, a nosy and well-intentioned woman. In either case, he wished that damn cloak did not hide her other assets. Was she a stick figure under that rough gray wool, or did she have curves to match that sweetly round face? She had fire enough in those tawny eyes of hers—at least she did when he poked at her—and she rather intrigued him.

Her hair, pulled back from her face into a knot of loose curls, was the same color as her eyes. The tawny color of a good Spanish sherry, in fact.

He'd always been partial to Spanish sherry.

"Bea, there you are. Oh, why must you always kitten here, you wretched animal." The words came out in such an affectionate cooing that he had to smile again. Sweet scolding indeed.

Then she turned away from the cupboard and demanded, her tone as prickling as a thistle patch, "Could you please bring the lantern closer? Bea is kittening."

He had been sitting there, swinging one booted leg, and now he stopped and stared at her. Who the devil did she think she was to be ordering him about in his own house?

Then she took off that awful cloak and poked back into the cupboard, stuffing it in there for her cat, and he forgot his affronted pride.

Thin blue fabric draped as shapely a rump as he'd seen on a female. Those curves made his hands ache and his mouth dry and his pulse skip to a happy gallop. He stared at her for a moment, then rose, took off his greatcoat, and brought the lantern up for a closer look.

She knelt on the floor, stuffing her cloak around a mewing striped cat and what seemed to be a mess of something sticky that looked rather like rats. He realized that he that looking at four newborn kittens, their eyes closed, their pink feet wiggling, and their ears not even standing yet. A fifth seemed to be on its way.

The mother cat—gray striped with white patches—mewed piteously and turned large yellow eyes up to its mistress's face. The animal's distress could not have shown more apparent if the creature could talk the king's English.

"Good Lord," he said, rather appalled at the situation.

Newell's cousin turned up a rather pale face to him. He couldn't blame her for that. New kittens and messy afterbirth did not seem a sight fit for any lady.

"Do you have any old handkerchiefs?" she asked, her voice anxious. "Bea's made something of a nest in the papers here, but she's having trouble with this one kitten, and she may need our help."

*Our.*

It took a moment for the word to settle in, and then he realized she had no idea who he really was or she would not have used such a harebrained word.

May need *our* help.

He was not a man who helped anyone—other than himself, thank you very much. And he had a hard enough time doing just that.

With regret, he glanced down at her sweetly curving rump, at her sherry-tawny curls knotted up over the white nape of neck. And then he put down the lantern, turned, and started for the door. "I'll send Knowles to you at once."

Emaline glanced up at Sir Ashten's retreating back, his wide shoulders so admirably set off by his coat, and his black soul so plainly shown by his callous disinterest in poor Bea.

If left to his own, the man would probably drown Bea and her kittens. But what else should she have expected from a hardened gamester, a man who, if Newell were to be believed—and he was generally not—had cheated at cards to win Adair Manor.

Well, she would not brand him a cheat, but she certainly could call him coldhearted and sinful.

Which was fine with her, she told herself. Better to know the worst of him at once, so that one could guard against the charm of his smiles. And she did not find him all that charming, she told herself as she turned back to helping poor Bea, or that handsome.

And she was such a bad liar, even to herself.

"There, there, sweet Bea. You've had dozens of kittens before this," she said, smoothing Bea's soft head and wishing she knew what else to do.

But the fear lay in her heart that perhaps Bea was getting too old to kitten, and that perhaps this would be the first kitten her sweet Bea would lose.

Half an hour later Knowles came back into the kitchen, wiping his bloody hands on a rag, his mouth downturned and his black eyes tired. Short and round, he wore his black hair shorn to nearly nothing, and he'd been with Ashten for so long that Ash could not clearly recall how he had gotten on before Knowles came to tie his luck to that of the Ravenhills.

"Well? Is she gone, and her cats with her?" Ash asked, looking up from the fire he had coaxed to life in the neglected hearth. He'd had to poke a broom handle up the chimney to clear the flue enough so that it would draw, and he had damn near ruined his coat in the process. However, he'd rather face a chimney than that woman. Chimneys never gave you accusing stares after you had disappointed them.

And then he added, unable to keep the words back, "Did the kitten die?"

Knowles gave a sudden grin, one gold tooth glinting in the fire and candlelight. "Wiff me there, sir? 'Course not. It may be touch-an'-go for a day or two, but the mite's a fighter. And it's Mrs. Pearson, sir. Mrs. Emaline Adair Pearson. She married the parson hereabouts, but he died five years ago, and she and her boys live at the gate house. She came here wiff her mother after her father died fighting some foreign war. Grew up in the big house here, it seems. And now, sir, we need a bit of milk for Bea, we do, sir. She's mortal tired, she is, and won't be up to rattin' for a bit. But Mrs. Pearson says her Bea's a fine mouser, and it'll be a good thing if she'll teach her little ones that for us here."

Ash stared at his manservant, a storm of emotions sweeping through him. Irritation at first to think his housebreaker married, then relief and interest to think her a widow—possibilities danced in his mind—and then back to annoyance that Knowles had found her so chatty and friendly.

His voice dry, he said, "That's a new record for you. A life of information in less than an hour."

Knowles shrugged his thick shoulder. "She's lonely, sir. And that worried about her cat. Had her Bea forever, she has, and greatly attached to her. Well, you know what females are."

Ash snorted and brushed the soot from his hands. "Don't I just. Well, where the devil will you find her that milk?"

"She said as I could ride to the Wiberforces next door and ask the squire for a pint of cow's own. We could use some for tea tomorrow in any case."

"I'd like to be fed myself," Ash said, frowning. "That is, if it's not too much trouble for you to remember you're my manservant, not that damn cat's."

"Aye, sir. But you ain't just had five kittens, and a

hard time of the fifth. Don't fret none. May as be I can cage us a few eggs for an omelet tonight." And before Ash could get out any more words of protest, Knowles slipped out the back.

"An omelet won't save you this time," Ash shouted out. But Knowles was gone already.

Muttering under his breath, Ash picked up a lit candle and made his way back to the library.

Knowles had lit a fire—the devil and Knowles himself only knew what he'd found to burn, or how he'd coaxed the chimney not to smoke. His pretty housebreaker still sat on the floor before the cupboard, her tawny hair tumbling down around her face, and talking soft nonsense to her cat as if it were a child.

Then she turned around and smiled at him, her face lit from within with a radiant glow.

His senses reeled under the impact of that smile as if one of the immense timber beams had swung down and clobbered him. It took him a moment to register that she had asked him something.

"The kittens? Do you want to see them?" she repeated, her smile faltering.

He scowled. He didn't want to see a litter of kittens. Instead, he gave a quick glance to the neglected, empty house. He had thought that at last he'd finally gotten ahead in the game, but he had only ended with a ruin and a litter of cats in his library.

He glanced back at his housebreaker, whose smile had faded into uncertainty. With a sigh, and all too aware that he ought not to act just to please her, he came forward to look at those damn kittens.

# Two

Emaline could not say why it was important for him to see the kittens. Perhaps it was that she wished to assure herself that he would not harm them. Perhaps she thought it would allow her better to judge just what sort of man now had control over her lease of the gate house.

Or perhaps it was as simple as that she wanted to share the sight of five tiny kittens, now cleaned by their mother's raspy tongue and nestled against Bea, their eyes closed slits, their fur fine as cut velvet, their little faces as innocent as Eden.

She opened the cupboard door a little wider and lifted the lantern.

Bea's eyes opened slightly, glittering like yellow diamonds. She opened her mouth but was too tired to even utter a protest. Beside her, five bodies wiggled, their noses poking Bea's belly, each seeking its own nipple to suckle. Tiny paws stretched. Thumbnails of tails curled. One black kitten with a white ring around his neck. One striped gray and white kitten, like Bea. One tortoiseshell kitten. One orange-marmalade kitten with white paws. One kitten gray as a morning fog.

Emaline glanced up to watch Sir Ashten's face as he looked into the cupboard.

There. In his eyes. She saw the faintest softening.

A wistful look that brought out the green. The lines around his mouth eased, so that the smile that curved that sensual mouth of his did not look so cynical.

A second later, all traces of that other man vanished. And he said, his tone sarcastic, "I shall have to make them a tour highlight when I show potential buyers about, and I will tell them, 'And here is the library, stocked with a goodly supply of cats.' "

Her hand tightened on the cupboard door, and she blinked up at him. "Buyers? You cannot be thinking of selling the estate?"

He glanced at her, his eyebrows raised and a challenge in his eyes. "I know it's a wreck of a house. But with luck—and if there's any blind men in the district—I shall sell Adair Manor for a tidy sum." He glanced around him. "Not, I daresay, for what it's worth—and certainly not the twenty thousand that your cousin stood it against—but perhaps with some paint, it might clean up well enough."

Panic pounding in her veins, she scrambled to her feet.

Ever since she had had Newell's letter, she feared this. Oh, Lord, what would become of her and the boys if they lost the lease of the gate house? Newell had also allowed the boys hunting rights on the estate. How would they get by without the game that the boys snared in the winter? And the fish they had from the river. A gamester was not the most desirable of neighbors, but she so had hoped he would at least be like Newell in being an absent landlord.

Instead, he wanted to sell.

Oh, drat him. And drat Newell!

Picking up her bedraggled cloak, she smoothed the worn cloth and said, her voice sharp, "Well, sir, I grant that the house is in disrepair, but that is easily remedied. And while most of the land is untenanted at the moment, it used to bring in a comfortable income of nearly nine hundred a year."

He gave a laugh, and then stood there, grinning at her. "My dear housebreaker, I'm more accustomed to bringing in nine hundred a night at the tables."

Her blush deepened, and Ash watched the color rise on her cheeks with appreciation. He did not add that there were those nights when he lost more than nine hundred, nor did he mention how the dice and cards could be fickle business partners. That, he judged, would give her too much cause for righteous argument.

Then he relented on his teasing and added, "But if you are worried about your cats, I shall make them a condition of sale. Or, you could buy the house yourself?"

Those tawny eyes clouded with trouble and a touch of hurt. What the devil had he said to seemingly wound her?

"Please, do not put yourself out over Bea and her kittens. I shall have them home with me in a few days. And now I bid you good evening, sir." And with that she swept out, taking her cloak with her and leaving him with a purring cat and five kittens.

He turned to them, pulling open the cupboard door to glance inside. Bea regarded him in turn with a steady glare that almost seemed to him to be accusing.

"I did not mean to upset her. And why should she not purchase the house?" He glared back at Bea and her kittens, and it occurred to him that his housebreaker's gown had been more than a touch out of fashion, and that her ancient cloak had seen better years. He had thought she had worn old clothes to go poking about a dusty ruin, but perhaps she had other reasons to wear such aged garments.

Bea let out a plaintive meow.

Ash's scowl deepened, and he told her, "You may yowl all you like, but I am not here to help you or her, or anyone but myself. So you may stay or go, but you had better not interfere with any sale of this house, you hear?" He stopped himself and glanced back to the empty doorway that Mrs. Emaline Pearson had strode out.

"Damn, but she's already got me talking to cats!"

"Mother! Mother!" The twin cries of greeting warmed Emaline's heart, and two boys tumbled into her arms as she bent down to hug them close.

She pulled back to ruffle Will's reddish-blond hair. A stout seven, Will had his father's pale blue eyes and a strong imagination. It was Will who made up the stories, but it was Thomas who led the two of them into trouble.

Just now, Thomas, a year older than his bother and a good half-foot taller, had dead leaves in his tousled dark brown hair and far too much innocence in his blue eyes.

She looked at him. "And what have you been doing?"

Thomas gave back a bland stare. "Nothing, Mother."

"We met a man," Will blurted out.

Thomas gave his brother a scowl. "We did not meet him. Least, not proper. He was only going through the woods."

Ignoring his brother, Will shifted to stand on one foot and bent his knee so that he could grasp his other foot and hold it. "He said Bea's had her kittens, and he was going to get her milk, and that he and a knight had moved into the big house. A knight named Sir Ravenhill," Will added, awe in his voice.

"It is proper to call him Sir Ashten," Emaline corrected. "And that must have been Knowles you met. He is Sir Ashten's servant. But you are not to go bothering our new neighbors. I do not want to hear that you have been to the manor."

Thomas's face tightened. "Can we not take Bea the kittening basket we made for her?"

"No, for I shall bring her home in a day or two."

"But why can we not go see her at the manor?" Will said, letting go his foot, his chin jutting forward with stubborn rebellion.

She opened her mouth to say that she did not want them near the influence of a hardened gambler, and then she realized that might sound all too exotic and tempting for two adventurous boys. So she said instead, her voice kept flat enough to make the whole issue sound boring, "Sir Ashten means to sell the estate and no doubt will be busy putting it to rights, so you should not bother him."

"Can we buy it?" Will asked, his eyes brightening.

*If only we could,* she thought, a fist of yearning clenching low in her stomach. If only she had more than eight hundred pounds to her name. And if only they did not have to live upon the interest that capital generated.

Rising, she changed the subject, for she could not trust herself to give an answer to Will that did not betray her own longing. "The question is, young sir, just what were the two of you doing in the woods today? Were you not supposed to be taking your Latin with Mr. Timothy?"

A scholar, Geoffrey Timothy had been a student of her late husband's, and in his memory had offered to tutor the boys two days a week. She was deeply grateful to him, for while she still hoped to persuade her starchy cousin Susan to pay for Harrow—or perhaps Winchester—for the boys, so far all she had from Susan were vague promises.

The boys glanced at each other. Will chewed on his lower lip, and then Thomas admitted, "He let us out early, so we went to see the fox den."

"The kits are almost grown," Will said, now hopping from one foot to the other.

She tried to frown at them instead of giving in to the smile that she wanted to offer. She had to be both father and mother, and she feared her own impulses to spoil and coddle them. So, her tone fierce, she told them, "Well, next time you are let out early, you are to come home first."

Thomas scowled at this restriction, but Will nodded, his eyes wide and his expression solemn.

Then she could bear it no longer, and she allowed a smile to soften her face. "And now, is that not fresh scones I smell baking?"

Both boys brightened and set off for the kitchen, jostling with each other, but with Thomas's longer legs gaining him a faster start to the kitchen.

Pulling off her cloak, Emaline folded it and laid it across the back of a chair. And then she glanced around her, seeing her home with the eyes of someone who knew that it was hers to lose, and with fear cold in her veins.

The cozy main parlor, the kitchen with its antiquated fittings, their infrequently used dining room, and the study that she had turned into a room for the boys to play in during bad weather. She thought of them all. Oh, how would they ever find such a good house again? Such an affordable house. Three bedrooms upstairs, plus the luxury of an indoor water closet, and space enough for Mrs. Cranley, who served as maid, cook, and housekeeper, to have her own rooms.

And that might be another knot to have to untangle. Mrs. Cranley had lived her entire life in the neighborhood. Her family lived here—not her husband, for "Mrs." was a title of respect. But she had two nieces with new babies, and an aging mother whom she looked after as well. If they must move from the gate house, would Mrs. Cranley come with them? And if they lost Mrs. Cranley, how would they ever replace her?

"Stop borrowing tomorrow's troubles," she told herself. But every instinct warned that more than the seasons were changing around her. And it was all due to that horrible Sir Ashten and his gambling ways.

Ash trod wearily up the stairs from the cellar, unbuttoning his waistcoat with one hand, and with a dusty bottle of something unlabeled in his other hand. He hoped it was brandy.

He had spent most of the day going over the house, attic to cellar. Thank the fates, it lacked a dungeon. It had, however, all the signs of a rat infestation, and years of neglect to undo. And what little else he had found had damn near made him want to pack up and turn his back on the whole place.

In half the rooms, what had once been silk wall coverings hung in tatters and would need to be stripped away. Most of the furniture had already been carted off, leaving hollow, empty rooms that gave Ash an uneasy chill in his soul. He had decided at once that Knowles must go into the nearest town to obtain the necessities—bedding, food, and something to sit upon that did not look as if it had been left over from William the Conqueror. He was not going to live in an empty cave of a house. Not even one he intended to sell.

And he could afford the furniture, thank heavens.

Stretching, Ash heard the kinks in his back pop. He was getting too old—or too soft—for cold nights on hard floors. There had been a time in his youth when he had been used to worse than this. But the years had been flush of late, and he had become accustomed to the luxury of feather beds, clean linen, and cheery fires.

Well, at least he had a big chair he could set before the library fire. And a bottle to sample. And some lively company to keep him amused.

He had poked into the library several times today, each time hoping to surprise his pretty housebreaker again. He had thought that he had heard the door open earlier, and her light step upon the floor. But either she had been quicker than he, or it had been his own wishes that he'd heard.

Instead, he'd found only Bea and her squirming kittens, their eyes still closed and their intent focused upon milk and naps. However, when he'd glanced into the cabinet, Bea had offered up a plaintive meow that had stirred him enough that he'd scratched her head. The mother cat's rumbling purr was oddly soothing, and he began to find a certain novel charm to having his own batch of kittens.

He had never had any pets before. Had never lived anywhere long enough to make it practical. And if the cat honestly was a good mouser, perhaps he should keep her and her offspring close by until she rid the house of its other unwanted guests.

He was thinking about just that as he opened the door to the library, and then he stood on the threshold, wondering who would be next to invade this damn house.

Two boys, close in age, sat cross-legged beside the kitten cupboard.

"I think Eber for the black," the older boy said.

The younger boy sat back, his nose wrinkling. Ash could not tell if it was with distaste or thought.

Then Ash interrupted, asking, "Just what sort of name is that for a cat?"

From their spots on the floor, the boys twisted around, twin expressions of alarm blanking their faces. Even in the fading afternoon's light, Ash recognized at once the tawny coloring of the smaller boy's hair, and he caught a familiar leonine slant to the older boy's eyes.

"You must be Pearsons," Ash said, strolling into the room. "You have the look of your mother as well as her habit for unconventional entrances."

The boys scrambled to their feet, the older one

clutching a cumbersome black leather-bound book and the younger one staring hard at Ash's boots until Ash glanced down himself to see why his riding boots so fascinated the lad.

"Mother said we weren't to bother you," the older boy stammered out in a nervous rush. "But we had to name Bea's kittens."

The younger one suddenly looked up at Ash, his face scrunched up with disappointment. "You don't have gold spurs."

His brother elbowed him, but the younger one merely glared at him and then turned back to Ash, his stare accusing.

Half amused and quite certain that he ought to chuck these two imps out by their collars, Ash knew they had caught him by his one weakness. His curiosity had been stirred.

"Spurs?" he asked.

"Real knights, like Arthur's, have them," the boy said.

For an instant, Ash stared back at him. *Arthur?* Then he almost let out a laugh. So the lad thought him a Knight of the Round Table. Had anyone ever been so misguided? However, the boy's intent expression stopped him from mocking such a mistake.

He bent down beside the youngster. "Yes, well, I can wear them only when I am summoned by the King to a state occasion, you know. Now, introductions are in order, I believe. I am Sir Ashten Ravenhill, Knight Commander of the Most Honorable Order of the Bath."

Straightening, he gave the boys an elegant bow, and saw that the flourish of his not very impressive title had made even the older boy's eyes widen. He'd never felt such an utter fraud before.

Recovering himself, the older boy gave a hasty bob of his head. "Thomas Pearson, sir. And this is my brother, William."

"Will," the younger boy said, frowning at his brother.

With a smile, Ash set a hand on Will's shoulder and turned with him to the cupboard. "Now that's done, tell me more about these names you are picking for our feline friends. I do feel as if I ought to have some say in the matter, since they were born in my house. And I rather fancy Misty as a name for the gray one."

Will drew back, shock on his face. "Oh, no, sir. That's not one of the begats!"

"Begats?" Ash asked.

Plopping down on the floor, Will reached into the cupboard to stroke a tiny furry head.

Thomas also sat down again, and Ash joined them, copying their style to sit cross-legged on the floor and wondering if his bad knee would allow him to get up again.

Opening the book he held, Thomas showed Ash the Bible. "See. We're already up to the third set of begats."

"Chapter eleven, Genesis," Ash read, eyeing the text with the uncertainty of one with too many sins on his soul to feel comfortable with the Good Book. "Well, Methuselah hardly seems a fit name for a cat."

"Oh, that was one of the better ones," Thomas said.

"Not like Ara-axed," Will added.

"He means Arphaxad, sir."

"Yes, but why such mouthfuls?" Ash asked. Then a thought struck him, sending an unhappy shiver along his skin. "Surely your mother's not all that pious? Is she a Methodist?"

"Oh, no, sir. It's because of Bea. You see, her name is really Begat," Thomas said.

Will squirmed and wiggled until he half lay on the floor. "Mother says that Bea came to the manor years ago. And had nine kittens in the library the night she came."

" 'Course that was before Will or I were born,"

Thomas said. "But Mother says that Great-uncle Walter joked that the cat was going to beget a house of cats. So Mother stared calling her Begat for all the kittens she had begot."

Looking from one of his narrators to the other, Ash's mouth twitched. So his prim housebreaker had a sense of humor. And was not so pious after all. Thank the Lord for that. He did not have a history that would appeal to pious ladies.

Glancing into the cupboard, Ash saw that Bea was busy washing her offspring. She hardly seemed to notice them, and the kittens were too intent on their next meal to mind. "Well, if tradition must be carried on . . ."

"Oh, it must, sir," Thomas insisted.

Will turned upside down so that he lay with his back on the floor and his heels resting up on the wall beside the cupboard door. "It must, Sir Ashten."

"It's Sir Ash to you, Sir Will. And, now, where are we with these names?"

# Three

Emaline stood on the steps to Adair Manor, caught between duty and propriety. She had been brought up to think of those twin masters of society before anything else. But which ruled in such a tangle as this?

She had knocked twice on the heavy oak door, hearing her thuds echo faintly in the nearly empty house. No one had yet answered. Should she leave? But how could she not check on Bea and her kittens? And how could she enter again without giving truth to Sir Ashten's accusations of her being a housebreaker?

Oh, drat the man for ever showing his face.

She shifted from one foot to the other.

The day had been a rare one for autumn—or would have been without this bother. A golden light lay in the afternoon sky as dusky purple gathered overhead. The air was as crisp and tangy as one of the apples from the stuffy Rustards' orchards, and a light breeze danced the dark red leaves from the branches of the beech trees. It was a late afternoon that called for a lazy moment to watch the setting sun. Or to use the twilight to steal an apple.

Instead, here she was, trapped on a doorstep, unwilling to go away and unable to go inside.

There was not a sign of life in the house—no smoke from any chimney, no light in any window. Had Sir

Ashten gone away again? At that thought the faintest disappointment touched her heart. She pushed down the treacherous stirring. She ought to wish the man and his devil's temptation of a smile gone. She had sons to raise and kittens to care for.

And that is just what she would do.

She hesitated only a moment more, and then she put her hand on the doorknob and let herself into the house.

Making for the library, she kept her steps light. Her heart pounded in her ears like thundering hoofbeats, and she winced at every creaking floorboard. Well, if anyone appeared to ask what she was doing here, she would say she had knocked and had thought them gone and could not allow her cat and kittens to be neglected.

However, instead of an accusing voice, she heard laughter and familiar voices coming from the half-open library door. She strode toward the sound, and then shock stopped her on the threshold as if someone had dumped a bucket of snow over her.

Sir Ashten Ravenhill, the notorious gamester, sat cross-legged on the floor, looking more like a schoolboy himself than a dangerous sinner. Next to him sprawled her boys.

An instant's fear flickered inside her for her boys, but it faded with the realization that all seemed innocent. And then irritation pricked in her chest that Will should look up at that man with such admiration glowing in his eyes, and that Thomas, usually so shy with strangers, should be chattering away about kitten names as if he had known this man forever.

She swept away her irritation at once with a proper determination to end this unseemly gathering. Will and Thomas had done wrong in coming here uninvited, and she could not allow that to go unremarked. Only she felt like the worst sort of hypocrite to blame them for doing what she had done herself.

And Sir Ashten . . . well, the man obviously had not an ounce of propriety or decorum in his body to be sitting on the floor with her boys in that fashion.

Clearing her throat, she strode into the room. Three pairs of eyes swung around to stare at her.

Will and Thomas scrambled to their feet, their expressions suitably hangdogged. However, the smile that lit Sir Ashten's fall-leaf eyes was anything but guilty.

That smile began as a deep and enticing glimmer in his eyes. Then it spread, lifting the corners of his wide, sinful mouth and relaxing the lids of his eyes. Emaline could only think that he should not look at her so in front of her children.

"Thomas, Will, come here at once," she said, her voice sharper than she had intended, but Sir Ashten had flustered her, and she hated that she might show him that he had done so.

The boys came, their steps heavy, and with Thomas complaining, "We did not bother him, Mother."

"We shall discuss that later," she said. Then she glanced back to Sir Ashten.

His smile had faded, and he stared at her, his eyes narrowed as if trying to puzzle her out.

That focused attention of his unnerved her even more.

She turned to the boys, tugging straight their collars, smoothing the wrinkles from their jackets, brushing at invisible lint. "You will please return home at once and wait for me in your rooms. Now, off with you. And it is to be straight home, mind. No side trips to any fox dens today, if you please."

She shooed them out the library door, but she did not look at them as they left, for she could not bear to see Will's drooping shoulders and Thomas's dejected scowl.

"They really were not bothering me, you know."

She swung around toward that beguiling voice. Oh,

how she wished she could blame him for this. But it was her own fault. She should have known that the boys would not be able to stay away from Bea's kittens any more than she could.

"Sir, I beg your pardon for these intrusions. Please be assured that I shall remove my cat and her kittens as soon as possible."

Still sitting on the floor, he propped his chin on his hand and his elbow on his leg. And she thought with irritation, *Has the man no manners that he cannot rise when a lady enters?*

"Mrs. Pearson, if that is an apology, then you are sadly out of practice. You've just begged my pardon with enough frost to put a permanent chill in this room."

She stiffened and glared at him. "Oh, I see. I am to show decent manners, while you lounge there like . . . like some decadent Eastern potentate!"

"Is that what's got your back up?" He started to rise, levering himself up by using the heavy chair for support. He got up on one knee, and then seemed to freeze as if caught by an invisible hand, and a soft mutter carried to her. "Oh, damn."

She had seen enough of her Uncle Walter's battles with gout to recognize a man in pain. And while she could not think that gout afflicted Sir Ashten, he had clearly stayed seated due to a physical difficulty.

She came to him at once, instinctively reaching for his arm. His hand clasped hers, and her own knees nearly buckled from taking his weight as he came to his feet. It was then that his strong arms steadied her, coming around her, grasping her, so that they swayed in an unsteady and awkward embrace.

For a moment, she allowed herself to stand there in the circle of his arms. Like a starving woman offered food, she could not help but reach for a taste, even if she should not. His arms felt so blessedly sheltering. A haven of strength.

*Oh, how long has it been since anyone's held me?* she thought.

And then she began to pull away, and she tried to make herself not want this by telling herself that it was all illusion anyway. He could not be such a gamester and be strong. Only weak men succumbed to such vice and sin. Men such as Cousin Newell. Her uncle had taught her that lesson well.

Stepping away from Sir Ashten's grasp, she smoothed her already smooth hair and said to him, her voice stern, "You have too much pride, sir. You obviously have a bad leg and ought to ask for help."

He grinned. "Lord, what a scold you are. You know, if you keep using that tone with your boys, you're going to turn them into the scourge of the neighborhood."

"I am not a scold," she said. Then she bit her lower lip, took hold of the ties to her cloak to knot them, and finally asked, "Do I really sound like one?"

"That tone would inspire any man to do his worst to live up to its condemnation. Why are you so harsh with everyone—yourself included? Haven't you had any happiness in your life?"

She glared at him, affronted. "Of course I have. I have the joy of two wonderful sons. And I was married to a man who loved me."

"But did you love him?" he asked, his voice soft.

Her mouth fell open. She struggled for an answer, found her mind empty, then decided that this conversation had gone beyond what two relative strangers ought to be saying to each other. Shutting her mouth into a prim line, she turned away so that she could look into the cupboard.

From inside, Bea stared back, her eyes half-slits, as if she really could not be bothered by all this human chattering. A good attitude to take, Emaline decided.

"That is not to the point," she said. "I came merely to see that Bea was doing well."

He let out a laugh and she straightened and turned around.

He leaned against the chair, his eyes alight with mischief and so knowing, so sure of himself, so teasing that her palm itched with the urge to strike the smile from his face.

"And I thought you came here for your boys. Why, you're no better than they are, stealing in for a glimpse of the kittens."

"I . . . I . . ."

"Come, you'll feel better for admitting the truth."

"Fine words from a . . . a gamester. And a . . . a cheat!"

The laughter died in his eyes. He strode toward her and she fell back until the bare shelves of the bookcase dug into her shoulder blades and she could move no more. He filled her view, and the heat from his body washed over her as if she had just opened a door to Hades. His eyes had hardened to green agates, and his jaw had taken on a daunting set. All she could think as her heart pounded was an inadequate *Oh my!*

His voice lashed at her as cold and sharp as the bite of an autumn wind. "Madam, I have few things in this world to call my own. I have the signet ring my father gave me when he wished me well on my sixteenth birthday and then set off with my mother for fresh horizons in the New World. I have the skin I was born in. I have my honor. So would you care to explain why you wish to strip the most precious of those possessions from me by naming me a cheat?"

Glancing down at her twisting fingers, she stammered, "I . . . I should not have said that. I do not really believe it. I am so very sorry."

His hand forced her chin up. "But *why* did you say it?"

She tried not to cringe, but memories flashed into her mind of her Uncle Walter's temper. She had never received its full weight, but poor Newell had. And even just being in the same room with that red-faced rage had left its mark upon her.

Now Sir Ashten's anger undid the last threads of her courage. She did not want to carry tales, but she could not stop the words that slipped out in a fast rush. "It was Newell's excuse as to why he lost the house, for he wrote to me that you had cheated him out of it in a game of faro, but I do not think he told that to anyone, it is just that he so hates for me to think badly of him."

And then she bit her lower lip to stop her rambling words before she said anything more.

Ash stood there, the anger hot in him, a round, soft chin in his grip and wide tawny eyes staring up at him. He gazed into those eyes and started to forget what it was he was supposed to be so angry about.

The heat remained, blazing in him, churning along with some other emotion too long neglected to be recognizable.

She was staring up at him, eyes frightened, but some other spark was kindling in those sherry depths. He knew hunger when he saw it in a woman's eyes. And an answering flicker of desire flared in him.

Lord, if she thought him a scoundrel now, what would she think of him if he kissed her soundly? And then he decided that he might as well find out.

He started to lower his lips to hers, and then a demanding yowl followed by sudden piteous mewing distracted him.

He glanced down to see Bea climbing out of her cupboard, leaving her kittens behind.

"What the—"

Mrs. Pearson slipped away from his touch, bending down to pick up her cat. "Oh, poor dear. She must need to go out. And you have fed her today, have you not? I shall just take her outside for a moment. Do mind the kittens and comfort them for just a moment."

And then she was gone. Ash turned to the five crying, forlorn kittens. He gave a frustrated sigh, then muttered to them, "Yes, and I know just how you feel to be so deprived."

He was gone when she brought Bea back. She heard male voices coming from the back of the house—Sir Ashten and Knowles, no doubt. She did not stay to take her leave, but saw Bea settled happily with her kittens, and then fled.

The boys waited dutifully in their rooms for her and their punishment for disobedience. But she had not the heart for it. Not after Sir Ashten's accurate assessment that she was as bad as they for sneaking over, and certainly not after his condemnation that she was a scold.

Oh, dear, is that what she had become?

As they sat down to dinner, she decided to try a new approach of reasoning with the boys about no more visits to the manor. But Thomas insisted that Sir Ashten had said they were welcome on his property anytime, and when Will asked if there was some reason they should not know Sir Ashten, Emaline did not feel up to giving an answer.

What could she say, after all? That he was a man who valued his honor? That hardly qualified as a reason for the boys not to know him.

However, she could not like his gambling for a living. And she had no wish for either Will or Thomas to start viewing that as a possible career option for themselves. So since she had no real reason to forbid the boys from calling on the manor, that meant she had to get Bea and the kittens home as soon as possible.

Three days later, the morning dawned warm and kind, another glorious autumn day, offering a memory of summer in its sunshine. A nip of cold lay in the air, enough so that Emaline bundled up the boys in wool coats before she sent them off with fishing poles and her blessing. Sir Ashten, after all, had said they were welcome. So she would take that as permission for the boys to continue fishing in the river that flowed across the Adair estate.

Then she took down her largest basket.

The kittens' eyes would be opening. They would be strong enough to come home. She longed to see the tiny furry creatures take their first glimpses of the world. And she wanted the boys to share that with her and with Bea.

And with the kittens home, there would be no reason for the boys to visit Sir Ashten. Then she would simply have to hope that he sold the house very soon.

On the walk up the drive to the manor, Emaline thought over all the possibilities of who might buy the estate.

She would not mind if Sir Ashten sold to Squire Wilberforce. He was a gentleman and would no doubt allow her to keep her lease of the gate house. However, the Wilberforces had no need of additional property to enhance their standing. And what if Sir Ashten sold to Lord Rustard? He was only a baron, but Lady Rustard took all too seriously her role as the "first lady" of the neighborhood. Emaline could easily picture them wanting a proper gatekeeper at the gate house, instead of a widow and her children.

The whole situation seemed be a choice between the lesser of evils rather than any goods.

And with that lowering thought, she mounted the steps to the manor.

As with her last visit, she pounded on the door at least five times, but this time her patience was rewarded. Knowles opened the door for her.

"G'day, Mrs. Pearson," he said, bowing her in. "Come to see your Begats?"

She sent him a questioning glance and he added, "The boys told Sir Ash about the name."

"Yes, well, you shall not have to be bothered any longer with them. I have come to take them home."

Knowles frowned. "To be quite blunt, Mrs. Pearson, I'd just as soon we could raise the mites. We could do wiff a bit of mousing. Prime hunting territory for the little ones, if you know what I mean."

"Yes, well, they are weeks from that age. But I shall see if the next owners perhaps would like to keep a kitten. Now, pray do not allow me to keep you from your work."

Knowles grinned, his wide face shining. "I was only chasing a spider out of the teapot spout. Would you care to take a spot of tea with Sir Ash now? It's no bother to tell him you've come for your cats."

"Oh, please don't. I mean, please do not bother. I shall be gone before you know it. And thank you so much for looking after them."

"No trouble at all, missus. Though I don't think he'll like you having taken them."

She frowned. "He cannot be all that attached to them."

Knowles gave a shrug. "Please yourself, missus," he said, then set off toward the back of the house and the kitchen.

Emaline frowned at him for a moment, then hurried to the library, determined to take her cats home.

Bea complained loudly as Emaline began to lift the tiny furry bodies from their mother's side. "I am only taking you home," Emaline told her. She rubbed Bea's soft head and then picked up another kitten. This one, the multicolor tortoiseshell kitten, had its eyes open, and wide blue orbs stared out of the black and orange face. It gave a faint mew. Emaline cuddled its downy cheek to her own. "You shall be quite safe, my darling. I promise. And you shall have a lovely bed in a basket near the kitchen fire."

With all five kittens in her basket, Emaline covered

it with a loose cloth. Bea wound around the basket, nosing it, meowing anxiously to her kittens.

And then a voice, low and teasing, said from the doorway, "First it was housebreaking, now stealing kittens. I fear, Mrs. Pearson, that there is no end to your sinful ways."

# Four

Ash sauntered into the room, a little surprised at himself.

He had thought to be glad to see the end of these pesky kittens. Oh, they were amusing enough. With their eyes open, they were starting to poke about—at least the black one had already tumbled out of the cupboard twice and had to be rescued and returned to its mother. Ash had already mentally christened him Trouble, despite the Pearson tradition for biblical names. Although he might yet allow Thomas and Will their way with Salah for the marmalade kitten.

But yesterday Ash had watched with disgust as Knowles constructed an earth closet of clay in one of the other empty library cupboards for the cats to answer nature's call. That alone, he'd thought, was incentive enough to see them transferred to the stables as soon as possible. Or anywhere else outside the house.

However, when Knowles had come into the kitchen and said that Mrs. Pearson was here to claim her kittens, a possessive streak of ownership flashed through Ash like a branding fire.

He did not want to give up his kittens. He certainly did not want to give up the only reason his pretty housebreaker had to visit him. The one maxim of his father's that he actually followed was that no reasonable man should deny himself a reasonable amount of pleasure. It was pure pleasure to taunt and tease his pretty housebreaker. And she was being unreasonable to attempt to deny him that.

"I suppose I shall just have to have you up before the magistrate," he said, coming toward her, his tone light and a smile in place for her.

She rose and held away her basket of mewing kittens, as if he were some sort of monster ready to devour them. The image amused him, and yet it also pricked him like a sword tip. Why did she think so little of him? What reason had she to be so self-righteous?

"Please, by all means do summons Squire Wilberforce," she said. "I should be delighted to have his assistance taking my kittens home."

He frowned. She sounded as if she held all the high cards in this deck. "Come now, Mrs. Pearson. You have no reason to remove your kittens. They are being well looked after, as you can see yourself by how they've grown."

She had the grace to color a little. Her cat wound around her ankles, calling up to its kittens with discontented yowls. Ash smiled. He thought he knew the ace to play. "Look, even your Bea objects to these relocation plans."

Her chin came up at that, and she fixed a hard look on him. "Bea is voicing a mother's natural concern for her offspring. Perhaps, Sir Ashten, since you do not have children, you do not understand a parent's anxiety. I have double that norm, for I must be both mother and father to my boys. It is a difficult thing, I assure you, but even you must understand my wish to guard them as much as I can from . . . from less than exemplary influences."

"You mean you do not think me fit company for them?" he said, unreasonably hurt by her condemnation. It was no more than he'd had from others in the past, but still it rankled.

Her tone and expression softened, and she put up a hand to push at the tawny curls that had struggled loose around her face. "It is not you, Sir Ashten. It is your profession. I grew up watching my cousin go from wild to worse. But to my sons, he always arrived at odd moments with armloads of presents and treats and high tales. And now I fear, with your knighthood and . . . and charm, that you will cement their notion that the life of the gaming tables is a viable future for them. Can you honestly say you would wish such a career onto a son of yours?"

He scowled at her, at those sherry eyes that pleaded for understanding, and he could only think that she had said that she thought he had charm. He tried to get past that thought, to fix on some reason not to let her take her kittens away.

But he knew well enough when he had lost a hand.

She had raised the stakes too high. For he would not wish his own life on any man—let alone on two boys who had indeed looked up at him with something near reverence in their eyes.

Damm it, but he envied her boys. They had a home—and a mother who'd fight for them like a lioness.

So all he could do was step aside and watch a grateful smile tremble on her lips before she dipped a curtsy and left, her kittens in a basket and her cat trotting alongside her swaying hem.

"Perhaps I should keep the estate and become a respectable gentleman?"

A rude snort answered Ash's musings. He turned away from the window and his view of a tangled, dying garden.

Knowles had discovered a bedroom at the back of

the house that had been left locked, and which had obviously been used for storage. Every damaged item—from chairs that wobbled to couches with torn upholstery to sticks of furniture suitable only for burning—had been dumped there. Ash dubbed it the "abandoned" room, and they were now sorting through what could be put back into service and what ought to be saved for the upcoming Guy Fawkes bonfire. Most of it, Knowles was convinced he could repair. Ash believed him.

Just now, however, he turned to his servant with arms folded and one eyebrow lifted in disdain. "Is it really so fantastic that I should wish to settle someplace at last?"

Knowles looked up from the side table to which he had been reattaching a leg. "How long have we lived in any one place? Even during the five-year King's service that gave you that respectable knighthood of yours?"

It was an irreverent answer, but Ash expected no less. They had been together long enough to be closer than most blood kin. "We spent an entire year in Venice," he said. "When I owned that gaming house."

Bitter, Knowles growled, "And what did you do but go and lose it? Had a nice house there, we did."

"I did not intend to lose it."

Knowles snorted again and turned back to his work. "How often does a bloody gaming house lose? Not unless it's bloody tired of being the house, now, does it?"

"Oh, you're simply still upset that we left Italy."

"Warm, sunny place, now, wasn't it? Only you wanted to come home, didn't you? That is, if England's a home to the likes of us. Spent only five years here, we did. And during most of that, you was too young to recollect much."

Smiling, Ash turned back to the view from the window. "Oh, I remember it."

He did remember. Faint, distant memories of a green lush world and a time before he had known what it was to be a roving gamester.

Adair Manor was all that he recalled of England.

The gardens near the house were a tangle of green and dying vines, but they would riot with color come the spring. Beyond that, green hedges and stone walls cut fields and vistas, carefully mapping out the surrounding property. He could see down the beech-lined avenue to the gate house, where a prim kitchen garden lay brown and fallow for winter. No doubt his thrifty housebreaker would plant potatoes and turnips for her winter crop.

In truth, he had played reckless that night in Venice two years ago. And relief had flicked in him when he'd lost the throw of the dice on which he had risked his entire fortune. Of course, without funds, it had taken them some time—and more games than he could remember—to make their way back to England. But a yearning had driven him to make the trip.

A deep, restless urge—but for what had he come?

For vague memories? For a lost past? For an illusion that he could be something he was not?

Already the familiar discontent had started to rise like shadows in his soul. He wanted something, but he could not put a name to his desire. That longing, however, had kept him up half the night in the library, practicing his card skills.

And he had not even a kitten to converse with, or to have watch the cards flicker past with wide, amazed blue eyes.

He started to turn away from the window, and then a flash of white caught his eye. Leaning forward, he stared out the window. What the . . . ? Was that a cat stalking its way to the house?

With a wry smile, Ash started for the door. "I'll be

in the library," he called out. But Knowles, engrossed in his work, only grunted back an answer.

Emaline came into the kitchen, her cloak folded over her arm. "Whatever you are cooking, Mrs. Cranley, smells divine."

Mrs. Cranley straightened from the pot she had been stirring. She cooked over the open hearth in the kitchen, managing to bake, fry, boil, and perform any number of miracles with this ancient art. Emaline could only be amazed, and while she might wish she could afford a new enclosed range, Mrs. Cranley scorned them as being impossible contrivances. "How can you tell what's a proper temperature without a flame to see?" she would say.

Wiping her hands on her starched apron, Mrs. Cranley gave a satisfied smile. "It's lamb stew. The boys came home with a shank from Mr. Timothy's larder, but what an odd fellow he is, to be sure, to think his lamb can do his courting for him."

Emaline smiled. Mrs. Cranley saw potential suitors for Emaline in every unattached gentleman in the neighborhood, whether he was nine or ninety. "Well, I certainly would rather a lamb shank than any number of posies."

She went over to the basket where they had settled Bea and her kittens. It lay empty, its dented cushion the only evidence that Bea had once lain there. Panic rose sudden and sharp. Where were the kittens?

Spinning around on her heel, she asked, "Where's Bea?"

Mrs. Cranley's face fell. "Why, she was here just a bit ago. Begged a bit of lamb from me, she did. When I was setting it to stew. You don't think—"

"Oh, I do think."

Grabbing up her basket, Emaline started for the

door. She did not even bother with her cloak. "Do not wait supper for me. I hope not to be long."

Ash watched fascinated as Bea carried her kittens back into the library cupboard one by one. He had opened the kitchen door for her and she trotted in, head up, kitten dangling from her mouth by the scruff of its neck, and the tiny creature half curled into submission. The kittens cried when she left to go and fetch the next of their number, so he stayed with them.

He sat in the enormous leather chair, piling the balls of fluff onto his lap, where they wobbled and stared about them.

When Bea brought the last of them—the black one—she crawled back into her cupboard and gave Ash an expectant stare as if to say, *You can put them back in with me now that we are home.*

He did so, and watched with a rather curious satisfaction blossoming in his chest as the kittens snuggled close to their mother for their next meal.

The expected knocking sounded on the front door all too soon. At first he thought he would allow Knowles to answer like a proper servant in a proper household. Then he remembered the broken furniture and Knowles's distraction, and so he went to the door himself.

"I have come for my cat and kittens," she said, and swept in like a duchess.

"Please do come in, Mrs. Pearson. Won't you take a glass of wine? I've discovered a tolerable port in the cellar, and we now have a daily supply of milk as well."

She halted and turned a startled stare on him, her red-gold eyebrows raised. "Milk?"

"The kittens put Knowles in the habit of acquiring a daily supply of the stuff. And since *our* kittens are having some themselves, I thought you might care to join them."

"Thank you, but no thank you." Hesitating, she bit her lower lip. "Are they really eating just now?"

"Come and see," he said, gesturing to the library.

Letting out a resigned sigh, Emaline followed him into the room and glanced into the cupboard. Bea lay there, looking contented, her purr a low rumbling. Five kittens lined up against Bea's gray and white belly, their faces lost in their mother's coat.

"Oh, Bea? Why must you always keep your kittens here?" Emaline said, unable to keep the exasperation out of her voice.

"Why indeed?" Sir Ashten said. "Please, will you at least sit down? We have acquired a settee, as you may have noted. And you really ought not to disturb them just now. So why do you not tell me about Bea's attraction to this particular room?"

He was playing on her conscience, she knew. And looking as smug as Bea did herself. However, he was right. She could not simply drag the kittens away from their mother just now.

She sat down on the settee, her basket on her knees. "It is not much of a story. Bea arrived at Adair Manor quite full of kittens, and before we knew what was what, she had her litter here. Of course, we tried to move them. Uncle Walter was not pleased to share his library. But no matter where we took her—kitchen, barn, my room even—Bea brought them back into this room. Eventually, even Uncle Walter gave in. And she has given us eight litters of kittens over the past eleven years. All in this same room."

He poured two glasses of wine into the mismatched goblets that Knowles had scavenged from a trunk from the abandoned room. "And do you really think that now you can convince her to keep her kittens with you at the gate house?"

She took the wine from him but did not drink. "I

must be more vigilant, that is all. If we watch her and do not leave open any doors or windows, she will have to stay."

He sat in the chair opposite her, looking amused and all too at home. And then she realized with a slight shock that was how he ought to look. This was his house now, even if he did not want to keep it.

Folding his hands before him, he asked, "Tell me, Mrs. Pearson, would you care to make a wager on whether you or Bea will be victorious in choosing where she raises her kittens?"

# Five

Emaline put her wineglass down on the floor and stood up, the comfort that had started to settle inside her now shattered. Anger flooded her veins, hot and quick, that he dared to offer her a bet. A bet. She felt as if he had slapped her face.

Voice shaking, she said, "I do not make wagers. And now I should take my kittens and leave."

He stood as well, placing himself between her and the kitten cupboard. "You need not take such a huff. I'm talking only a friendly wager, nothing more. Or are you so righteous that you allow no pleasure to enter your life?"

"There are many things that offer pleasure that do not involve gambling."

He smiled at her, his eyes more green than brown, and the suggestion of very pleasurable things lay like an invitation in that smile. All innocence, he asked, "Do you mean such things as kisses out of doors on a crisp autumn day? Or snuggling before a fire while the rain pelts down? Or a warm—"

"I mean none of those!"

His smile widened, and his eyes took on a mocking glint. "What? You've never enjoyed the pleasure that God designed for man and woman to share?"

Cheeks flaming, she tightened her stranglehold on

her basket and her temper. "Sir, allow me to tell you that you are an unprincipled rogue. You taunt me. But I shall not allow you to torment me into making my cousin's mistakes. I was seventeen when my mother came to me and explained that a London Season would be impossible due to the heavy debt placed on the family by Newell. I did not mind, but I did mind the heartache and worry his excesses caused my aunt and uncle. And if you ever dare suggest any sort of wager to me again, I shall be quite happy to box your ears for such impertinence! Now I bid you good day, and I shall come to collect my kittens on the morrow!"

And with that she turned, her blue skirts swirling around her heels, her chin up and her color high.

As the front door slammed behind her, Ash let out a soft whistle. Lord, what a firebrand. A good thing he was selling this house, for if they had to live as neighbors, they would end scratching at each other like two wildcats.

Pity, though, that a comely widow such as her didn't know how even to flirt, let alone carry on a light dalliance. And he certainly would not have minded instructing her in that art.

The following morning Emaline collected Bea and the kittens early enough that she could avoid an encounter with Sir Ashten. She thought herself safe from him until the very next day, when Mrs. Cranley left open a window through which Bea made good an escape. When she went kitten collecting a second time, she thankfully found Sir Ashten was out again and had to deal only with Knowles.

The day after, however, it was Will's fault, for he had not fully shut the door behind him when he left the house for his lessons. So for a third time in as many days, Emaline found herself trudging through crunching brown leaves, her nerves worn and her thoughts tumbling.

Would she have to see him this time? What would he have to say to her? Oh, why had she been so rude? And why had he been so . . . so . . . so much a rogue!

The wind stung cold on her cheeks and brought to mind the images he had planted, which had swirled inside her like a fever dream.

What would it be like to have his warm lips on hers with a brisk autumn wind stinging her face? And how would it feel to have his arms strong around her and the trees whispering secrets just as their hearts were?

She shook off such fantasies, angry with herself and even more so with him. What a devil to have suggested such things. And she was an even worse sinner to dwell on them. Well, she would stop thinking about it. And in a few more weeks the kittens would be grown and Bea would stop bringing them back here. Or he would sell the house and be gone.

Only why was it that either thought lay heavy as a weight on her heart?

Feet dragging, a tight band of nervousness around her chest, she mounted the stone steps of Adair Manor and plied the brass knocker, now brightly polished.

Knowles answered her summons and bowed her in with the news that she had managed yet another reprieve. Sir Ashten was out.

"He's walking his property," Knowles said as he shut the door against the chill of an early October day.

Instead of feeling relieved, irritation stung her. Out again. Could the man not stay put anywhere? She could not stop from saying, her tone sharp, "Judging the value that he might get from it, is he?"

She blushed at her own poor manners, but Knowles merely shrugged and said, "More like gone off to think himself five and with a home again."

His answer made her turn and stare, puzzled. She ought not gossip with Sir Ashten's servant. But curiosity stirred, wiggling like a hungry kitten that would quiet down again only if fed. So she asked, striving for a casual tone, "Do you mean to say he has not had a home since he was five?"

Knowles led the way into the library, talking as he went, and Emaline listened to his story, astonished, a little horrified by the tale.

It seemed that Sir Ashten had been born to a gambling father and a mother who doted on her husband above all else. Knowles himself had gone into service with the family just before Mr. Ravenhill lost the family home in a wager, resulting in that gentleman setting off for the continent with his wife, his son, and Knowles to look after the boy.

"It were lean years back then. Never more than a few weeks in any place," Knowles said, picking up a furry gray kitten and settling it into Emaline's basket.

"How awful to be so shifted about," she said.

"You don't miss what you don't know, missus. But there were times I'd catch him staring into a family's window, watching them act like a family. 'Course, matters weren't helped that Mr. Ravenhill, well, he were rather too fond of making sure the luck ran in his favor, if you know what I mean. 'Course, Ash wouldn't have nothing to do wiff such tricks."

Blinking, she stared at him, then realization dawned. "His father cheated?"

"Not regular like. But enough that it led to them parting harsh like. We joined up and was off for India when his parents booked passage to the Americas. 'Course, Ash had to add a couple years to his age to take up the king's shilling, but he was tall for his years. He got himself that knighthood for his service, but we didn't care much for India. Blisterin' hot it were."

Emaline added the last kitten to the basket. She sat on her folded knees, stroking Bea's head, seeing in her mind's eye a boy on the verge of manhood, gangly and proud. A man who had won his knighthood the hard way—with his own blood.

"Is that why he left the army?" she asked. "Because he . . . well, because he disliked India?"

"Oh, no, missus. Got a saber in his leg, he did. After that, what could we do but take up the cards again. The luck don't always run our way, but we done well enough."

He glanced around the room, his round face pulling down into a frown. " 'Course, this was supposed to be our windfall. Supposed to retire on this. Don't suppose that'll happen now."

Emaline rose and picked up her basket. She tried to remember that whatever Sir Ashten had been in the past, that lost boy, and that solider, had turned now into a hardened gamester. She really should not feel sorry for him.

"Yes, well, I am certain Sir Ashten will find someone who wants to buy the estate."

A deep voice answered from the doorway, "I believe I already have."

Emaline turned to see Sir Ashten, his hair windblown and color stung into his sun-warmed face. He smiled as he came forward, but a challenging glint in his eye left her wondering how much he had overheard. She itched to ask whom he had found to buy the estate, but she burned with guilt already for the impertinence of having been caught gossiping about him.

After a wink to Emaline, Knowles ambled from the room, saying, "Appears I'm wanted elsewhere, missus."

Ash turned to his guest, inwardly cursing Knowles's prattling ways. He disliked having his past trotted out like some novelty meant to amuse. Then he noted the worry clouding his pretty housebreaker's eyes, and his mood softened.

Over the past few days he had glimpsed Bea carrying her kittens to the manor, hauling them along by the scruff of the neck. Each time Emaline had strode up the drive, coming for them like an avenging angel to save a damned soul.

After their last encounter, he had thought it best to keep his distance and had left Knowles to deal with her. But now that he had her before him, he changed his mind.

He had missed her. He had missed teasing the temper into those sherry-brown eyes. He had missed her sharp edges and smooth curves. He was in need of diversion. And he wanted it with her.

He glanced down at the basket and the kittens struggling to climb out, their pointed faces poking out from under the covering of a blue and white checked cloth. She kept pulling loose their claws from the wicker and setting them back under the covering.

"You know, this really must stop," he said, trying not to smile at the kittens' persistent escape attempts.

She frowned. "I am trying to keep Bea with me, and if I can . . ."

"I don't mean that she must stop bringing them here. I mean you must stop taking them away. The weather's about to turn. My leg always lets me know about that. Do you fancy giving those little mites a soaking? And what if Bea tries to venture out at night? I certainly don't want to go walking and find that some fox has make a snack of a kitten."

She glanced down at the basket, her forehead bunched tight, and he saw that he had breached her defenses at last.

With one hand he scooped up the black kitten as it tried to climb out of the basket. He held it to his chest, feeling its purr rumble through his coat and shirt. "Mrs. Pearson, let us strike a deal."

"I do not—"

"No, do not interrupt. And you may stop looking daggers at me. I mean an honest bargain, not a wager. Let us allow Bea her way and her kittens the cupboard. And while they are here, I vow to keep it respectable enough that you may visit without a qualm. There shall be no gaming, no vice . . . not even so much as a dancing girl," he said, unable to resist adding the last.

She glanced at him from the corners of her eyes, wary but calculating, and he wished suddenly that she did play cards. He would wager now that she would play cautious but well, weighing her moves and shrewd with her actions.

"What if you sell the house?" she asked. "You cannot promise the next owners will be so generous with their rooms."

"Then I promise not to sell until the kittens are grown. What does it take? Six weeks?"

"Twelve. Bea has to teach them to hunt, you know. But you said that you already had a buyer."

"I have had an offer, but one so low that it has convinced me I must do something to at least put a pretty face on this place if I am ever to be rid of it for even half its value. So let us say eight weeks, then, from the day they were born."

"Eleven from a week ago," Emaline said, and wished she had the courage to ask him who had made the offer and how much it had been. But that went beyond what was polite to ask.

With the black kitten climbing his coat to his shoulder, he held out his right hand. "Agreed."

Emaline stared at the tapering, elegant hand. Those long fingers were capable of manipulating cards, shifting them to do his will. Was he also manipulating her? Well, it did not matter. A ten-week reprieve was still a reprieve from an uncertain future.

She looked up at his face again. The black kitten had curled up on his shoulder, happy, as if it had found a new home, its face pressed into the strong column of his neck. If a kitten could find it in him to trust Sir Ashten, perhaps she could as well. Just a little.

Slowly, she put her hand into his. His face relaxed into a smile as his fingers closed around hers, his touch warm, his grip gentle but strong. His thumb brushed across the back of her hand, drying her mouth to dust.

She pulled away at once with the excuse of kittens to deal with, too aware of him, of his strength, of his person. Bea was making little noises at the back of her throat, calling to her kittens, and it gave her an excuse to move away.

"I had best put them back, I suppose," she said, bustling to do so, wondering if he had this effect on all women, or if too many years of widowhood had left her particularly susceptible.

"There's still one more matter to settle," he said.

She had knelt beside the cupboard, and now she glanced up at him. "What matter?"

He came over to her, kneeling so close that she could smell the damp of a light rain on his wool coat and see the fine stubble that shadowed his cheek.

Plucking the black kitten off his shoulder, he placed it with its litter mates, his hand brushing hers as he did so, leaving her thoughts scattered and the room suddenly warm.

And then he asked with a smile, "Must we really give these kittens of ours biblical names?"

They started through names the next night. Sir Ashten insisted that Emaline and her boys come for dinner to seal their bargain and christen the kittens. He promised there would be a table to eat upon—it had been too large to remove—and said they had hired some temporary help from the village.

Temporary.

The word carried a good reminder of Sir Ashten's habits. He drifted like the leaves on the wind, blowing away with the seasons. It also carried the ominous warning of her uncertain future. And then it occurred to her to wonder if she could possibly convince Sir Ashten to sign a lease that would be binding upon the next owner as well.

# Six

Her chest tightened at the idea of having to ask Sir Ashten for anything. After all, why should he deal kindly with her? She certainly had not done so with him. She had judged him by the low standard of her gamester cousin, giving him no chance to prove himself.

Of course, he was not a complete gentleman. How could he be with his past? But all she knew of him to date spoke of at least an honorable man. A man who made his living from cards, but who did so honestly. And while he might tease her, he had shown kindness to Bea and her kittens. That spoke well of him.

Only he had no reason to sign any sort of binding lease with her. She had not even the knowledge if such a lease could be made legal. *Oh, John, why could you not have been a more worldly man so that you left me and the boys better able to deal with this world?*

With a sigh, she set aside thoughts of her late husband. He had indeed been a good man. But not a practical one. It seemed, instead, that she must always be practical.

Which meant that she would have to do what she could to mend her relationship with Sir Ashten, so that she might then be able to ask him about the possibility of a more binding lease of the gate house.

With that in mind, she dressed for dinner in her best evening gown, a white muslin with silver and blue silk embroidery that she had not worn in three years. It still fit, though its train dated the style terribly, and the bodice pinched in and pushed up her breasts in a rather shocking fashion. She tugged up the dress as much as she could, and then donned her mother's necklace of blue enamel and gold. She dressed Thomas and Will in their good dark-blue suits, though Will wiggled dreadfully when she tried to brush his hair into charming curls. Settling for his having a clean face, and for Thomas looking remarkably like his father, they set out for Adair Manor in the pony cart.

The Findleys' eldest son, Rob, met them at the house to take the cart around to the back. Emaline's stomach fluttered as much as it had when she was a girl going to her first ball. But she took a breath to steady herself and then herded the boys up the steps and into the manor.

It seemed transformed.

The hall glowed with polished floors and candlelight. A table she had not seen since her girlhood stood in the center of the square room, and a floral tapestry—moth-eaten on one corner—hung opposite the fireplace.

She glanced around her, startled by the change and oddly pleased to see the house look so welcoming again.

"Knowles and I have been busy today, so you'll have to excuse me if I fall asleep by nine before the fire," Sir Ashten said as he came down the stairs.

She turned to greet him, and the polite words she had ready caught on her heart and wrapped tightly around it. She had thought him handsome with his shaggy sun-drenched hair and his beautiful clothes so carelessly worn. She had not known the half of it.

His forest-green coat brought out the green in his eyes. His close-fitting clothes set off the width of his shoulders and emphasized his narrow hips. Brushed and golden, his hair lay smooth from his face, and the fire and candlelight drew glints from the warm depths.

She had time to study him as he bent to answer a question from Will and then turned to bid good evening to Thomas, and it struck her that for a gamester, he had an uncommonly strong jaw. A lovely jaw that ended in a square, stubborn chin.

Then he glanced up at her, that sensual mouth of his quirking, and mischief sparking in his eyes, and she knew that she had been caught in her study of him.

He said nothing. No teasing comment. No tormenting suggestions about the intent behind her close observation. He merely acted like the gentleman he looked, saw to Knowles taking their wraps and then bowed them into the dining room.

Dinner passed easily.

Ash strove to be a courteous host and bit the inside of his cheek a dozen times to keep back the seductive phrases he wanted to lavish on his pretty housebreaker, and which would have her frowning at him instead of smiling. She ought to be flirted with, however. That low-cut gown set his imagination working feverishly as to what she would look like without it, and challenged his self-control not to find out.

Thank heavens for the boys. They chatted on about their lives—about fox dens, lessons, neighbors, fishing, and hunting—so that conversation never lagged.

Knowles had outdone himself in the kitchen, producing oxtail soup, fish pie, jugged hare, celery with cream, stewed peas, and baked apples with custard. The boys tucked into the last as if they had not eaten heartily of the other dishes.

As they quit the dining room for the comfort of the library and the kitten naming, Ash held back with Mrs. Pearson and asked, "Do they always eat like such good trenchermen?"

"Yes, and I am afraid they are rather like the river carp—the more I feed them, the larger they become."

"You shall have giants on your hands."

She looked up at him, a smile dancing in her eyes and her lips curving, and something gave an odd twist in his chest.

But then her boys called to her to come see Bea, and she moved away, breaking the moment.

He stared after her, frowning, not quite certain what had just happened. He knew well enough what it was to fall in—and out—of love. He had done so a dozen times or more. And she was certainly attractive enough to stir more than lust in any man. But this . . . this sudden protective desire was a new thing. In that instant he had not wanted her in his bed as badly as he had wanted with a fierce passion to keep her safe from anything that would rob her of that rare smile of hers. The problem was that a gamester such as himself was one of the things most likely to steal that smile away.

What a damnable tangle.

"Sir Ashten," Will said, interrupting Ash's thoughts. "Do you like Rue or Peleg better?"

"Peleg," Thomas said at once, dancing a string before the gray kitten who lay with its litter mates on the carpet before the fire, its eyes dominating its pointed face.

Ash came over to them, and the naming began in earnest.

Half an hour later, not one kitten had been christened. However, Ash had a far better idea of Mrs. Emaline Pearson's personality and her situation.

She and her Bea were both fondly protective of their offspring. Ash found it amusing that both kept an indulgent but watchful eye on the events, occasionally reaching in to smooth a tousled curl or in Bea's case, to lick a spot left sticky by one of the boys after cakes had been brought in by Knowles.

From the comments dropped, Ash gathered that his pretty housebreaker lived on scant funds, taking in sewing to supplement her income, and that the boys hunted the estate as a much-needed source of food. It troubled Ash to think that they would lose that when he sold the place, so he turned his thoughts away from such unpleasant things.

The boys were also getting to that age where they needed male guidance. He noticed the resentful looks that Thomas shot his mother when she treated him as if he were as young as Will. He was a good lad, but Ash saw the burning desire in Thomas to be given more responsibility and to be recognized more as an adult.

Ah, but that was not his problem either.

As the arguments over names ranged—with Thomas insisting they must use the begats, and Ash arguing against that mostly for the sake of arguing, and Will torn between—Emaline sat and listened to them. And Ash watched her watching them.

Finally, in a moment of quiet, she said, "Well, why do we not give them two names?"

Ash grinned. "Ah, the wisdom of Solomon and the beauty of the Queen of Sheba. What do you say, lads? Shall we honor the lady's request?"

Emaline gave him a warning look, but she did not rebuke him for his compliment.

Will scooped up the black kitten, who had been chasing the gray kitten's tail. "I want to name him Sir Lancelot, and we'll call him Sir."

"We said his name was Eber," Thomas said, scowling.

"You said it. I didn't."

"And I said his name was Trouble, which is just

what he's proving to be. What, Oh wise lady, is your just decision on this matter?"

Emaline realized that three sets of eyes now turned expectantly in her direction. She opened her mouth, shut it, and then said the first thing that popped into her brain. "Call him Sir Eber Troublealot du Lac."

Eyes dancing, Sir Ashten regarded her. "The name is bigger than the kitten, but perhaps he'll grow into it. Do we all agree on this one?"

Sir Eber was now batting at Will's cravat and untying it, but Will looked pleased to have a knightly kitten. Thomas, still frowning, looked ready to argue, but then he glanced at his mother and relented with a nod.

From there the naming went quickly, but by the end of it the suggestions had become so absurd as to leave Will giggling, and even Thomas gave up a few reluctant smiles. The marmalade kitten became Lady Sheba Salah, and the striped kitten Sir Nahor Galahad. Lady Peleg du Mist was settled on for the gray, and in the end all they could come up with for the tortoiseshell kitten was a simple biblical Reu, which pleased Thomas.

Within a week use had shortened the names to Sheba, Sir Eber, Lady Mist, Galahad, and Reu. And Ash found that he was becoming dependent upon the company of his pretty housebreaker and her offspring.

That was born in upon him one rainy day when the drenching weather kept Emaline and her boys away. Ash prowled the manor, restless as a caged bear and almost as cross.

Trying to contain costs, he had not undertaken any major work but had settled for painting rooms, replastering ceilings, replacing missing stones from the exterior, and putting new lead on the roof. But what he saw still displeased him.

The house was coming back to life, and it made the bleak, tangled gardens look worse. Everywhere seemed to be scaffolding, cloth coverings, and more disorder than order. What had he gotten himself into?

His mood dark, he drifted into the library and threw himself into the leather chair that sat before the dying fire. How was he to ever sell this place for a decent price? Lord Rustard had made a ridiculous offer of two thousand pounds, a sum not even a quarter of what the property should fetch. Had he been wrong to turn the man down? Was he only wasting his capital by making these repairs?

He certainly didn't mind risk, but he disliked that he did not even know the odds of this game. He wondered now if the few hundred he had sunk into the house would turn into a few thousand, and for what? For getting his own money back?

Or for the smiles that transformed Emaline Pearson's face when she saw the rooms renewed and the house repaired?

What the devil was he doing?

A curious black face poked out of the cupboard, followed by a pointed gray face. The pair of kittens tumbled out, pushed forward by their litter mates. Ash had to smile as the bits of fluff stared around themselves, sniffing the air before they ventured to his side.

"Questing already?" he said, scooping up the gray, who lifted her chin for a scratch and set to a rumbling purr. Sir Eber would not be caught, however, and darted off to lurk under the sofa, with only an occasional black paw lashing out at dust motes.

Ash grinned. Tiny furry clowns, the kittens amused him, lightening his mood and making him wonder if indeed he ought to reconsider keeping the house. But he knew all too well his status in the neighborhood. Lord Rustard certainly had made it clear with his hints that a man like Ash would not be welcome into the society of a small community. Indeed, the only visitor to the manor had been his pretty housebreaker.

So he could not stay. Not unless he could somehow

convince the community that he was a leopard who had shed his spots. Or unless he cared to become a hermit.

Which meant that he ought to leave, and sooner rather than later. October was nearly spent, after all, and today's rain foretold the winter to come. Better to leave with the roads still decent enough to travel. And Knowles might like going back to Italy.

He sat there, lost in his thoughts, until a frightened mewing caught his ear. Sitting up, he listened. Lady Mist still lay on his lap, but what had become of Sir Eber Troublealot? Was that damnable kitten living up to his name?

Bea had also heard the faint cry, for she came out of the cupboard and streaked for the door.

Following, Ash tracked the cat and the cries into the drawing room and saw at once that Sir Eber had stranded himself.

They had put up scaffolding to repair some of the plasterwork on the ceiling, and the kitten had clawed its way up a rope that dangled from the topmost planks. Sir Eber now hung from his front claws, swaying slightly, mewing in panic, and utterly trapped. The kitten could not let go of the rope without falling more than twenty feet to the bare wood floor. And the tiny kitten lacked the reach and agility to climb off the rope and onto the scaffolding.

With a curse, and a shout to Knowles, Ash put down the gray kitten, leaving it beside the yowling Bea. Then he started up the scaffolding himself. The boards creaked under him, and he spared a thought to wonder if they would support his weight; they had been built for and by two spry, elderly workmen from the village. But then Eber lost his grip on the rope with one paw, and Ash knew he had no time to lose. He ran up the ladders, ignoring the dangerous swaying of the structure, and reached out just as the kitten lost its grip.

The black kitten fell into his outstretched hand, and

then Ash froze. Scaffolding swayed. Slowly, carefully, Ash started down.

"What the bloody hell you doing up there?" Knowles said, coming into the room.

"Amusing myself. Be a good fellow and steady that ladder," Ash said, and just as he did, the plank under his foot snapped.

He caught himself on the rope as he fell, snagging it with his one free hand. Hemp tore into his palm, making him swear, and then a sharp jolt of pain sang into his shoulder. Tears mixed with stinging sweat, which flowed into his eyes. Agony blazed across his shoulder. Something had tore loose.

"I'm coming up," Knowles shouted.

"Don't you dare!" Ash said between clenched teeth. "If it won't hold my weight, it won't hold yours."

"Then I'll get help."

"Excellent suggestion," Ash muttered, but he had already heard the front door slam as Knowles left the house at a run.

Knowing that he could not long hang there, Ash glanced about and then gently swung himself. Each move stabbed searing pain into his shoulder, but at last he managed to swing far enough to wrap his feet around one of the scaffold poles. Sweating and now almost sick from the effort, he got himself half perched on a narrow plank that sagged ominously.

He sat there, dizzy with pain, a terrified kitten digging its tiny claws into the back of his hand. Then the door slammed again, and when he straightened, Ash realized that he now had an audience.

"What the devil do you two think you're doing?" he called down.

"We're here to help, sir," Thomas said, his hair and coat wet from the rain.

"They're light enough to come up," Knowles shouted.

"I'm not having—" Ash started to say, but a jab of

pain cut off his words, and in the next second Will and Thomas were already scampering up the scaffolding like two monkeys.

Will reached him first and Ash thrust the kitten at him. "Here. Take him down and yourself with him."

Taking the kitten, Will hesitated. But then Thomas arrived and said, "Go on, Will. And best help Mr. Knowles pad the floor. Now, Sir Ash, can you climb?"

His palm burned like blazes, his shoulder felt as if it had been wrenched out of his socket, but Ash managed a crooked grin. "I am only almost as helpless as poor Eber. Come and lend me your shoulder, and let us hope we do not need that padding."

Will and Knowles had been dragging in every pillow and blanket in the house, but in the end Ash made it down without falling. With his good hand freed from having to hold the kitten, and Thomas testing the boards for him in advance, the progress was painfully slow.

When they reached the floor, Ash slumped onto the pillows and found that to be even more uncomfortable.

He started to sit up, swore at what it cost him to do so, and then a blast of cold air told him he had yet another visitor.

"Oh, damnation," he muttered, and glanced up to see Emaline Pearson in the doorway.

# Seven

“I thought you said this would be a respectable house while the kittens were here,” Emaline said, coming forward and undoing the ties to her rain-darkened cloak. A teasing tone softened her words but did not hide the worry in her eyes.

Ash managed a grin and then winced and held his shoulder. “A man ought to be able to mutter a much-needed curse in his own house.”

She came to kneel beside him, her hair slicked back against her damp, pale face and her eyes dark and wide.

“You are wet,” he said.

“And you are injured. Thank you, Knowles, for leaving word with Mrs. Cranley that you were bringing the boys here.” She glanced up at the scaffolding and took Ash’s injured hand, turning it to expose his rope-burned palm. “What foolish nonsense were you thinking to climb up that after a kitten?”

“Well, I am a knight, after all. It seemed a good day to rescue fair kittens in distress.”

She frowned at him and then reached up to touch his shoulder. When he winced and tried to pull away, her worry clouded to fear. “Oh, you have done yourself a harm. It’s not just your hand, is it? No, you are to stay still. Knowles, please fetch Dr. Pritchard.

Thomas, go with him and show him the way. Will, go and ask Mrs. Cranley for her cucumber salve and the friar's balsam tincture that she uses for her joints."

"Yes, ma'am," three voices echoed at once.

Ash lay back on the pillows, wincing as his shoulder warned him to take care. "I see I am in formidable hands."

"Well, it seems to be my day to rescue knights in distress, Sir Ashten. Now tell me where it hurts."

He grimaced as she touched his shoulder again, and she immediately pulled away. "I do not wish to alarm you, but I think you have dislocated your shoulder."

"I don't wish to alarm you, but I know I have. I've done so once before, and I was warned it could happen again. It's got to be put back, and the sooner the better. Have you ever done such a thing?"

"Should we not wait for the doctor?"

"If you are squeamish, dear lady, we shall wait. But I can tell you from experience that it'll feel far better when it's back in place, and the longer it's out, the more it stretches parts that should not be stretched. Oh, damn."

Emaline winced, and not at his curse. Every time he moved, even a fraction, he seemed to be in pain. She could not stand to see him so. Taking hold of her courage, she drew in a breath, then said, "What must I do?"

He gave her instructions on how she must pull his arm out to pop the joint into place, and then he offered up a crooked grin. "It will hurt me far more than you, so you'd best give me something else to think about while you do it."

"Give you what? Brandy?"

"A kiss. Just for distraction." He reached up with his good hand to caress her cheek, brushing at her damp skin. "Come now, no one is watching, and instead of slapping me afterward, you can pull my arm until it aches."

She started to protest, but his hand had slipped to the back of her neck and he was already pulling her close. Her lips parted with unvoiced reasons why she should not kiss him, but she let him draw her to him anyway, her chest tight and her skin tingling. His eyes seemed black pools that would drown her, and his hand urged her to what she had ached for in her dreams.

And then his lips brushed hers and she forgot that she was kneeling on a pillow-strewn floor and kissing a gamester.

Warm and soft, his lips touched hers like a summer sun. Her hand stole up to his face to trace the curve of his jaw, to tangle in the silk of his hair. She let out a sigh, and then something furry and sharp pounced her hand.

Pulling back, she found Sir Eber attacking her hand and Sir Ashten's hair. She untangled the kitten from Ash's sun-lightened hair as he glared at the wiggling black body.

Then he smiled up at her. "Best do it now, for after a kiss such as that, I could die a happy man."

And so she set aside the kitten, took his injured arm, and pulled, only it was she who wanted to cry out as she saw the pain twist his face.

Afterward, with his shoulder in place, he lay still, white lines bracketing his mouth, and she needed to do something to ease his suffering. So she leaned close to him, her chest against his as she caressed wisps of warm brown hair from his face. This time she brushed her lips across his without his urging, and then she pressed her mouth to his damp temple, and smoothed his face, and wished she could do far more than this.

Oh, but the man tempted her to folly.

He stared up at her, his eyes unfocused and heavy with pain, but he smiled anyway and said, his voice a rough whisper, "You make me long to be something I'm not, my pretty housebreaker."

Through his waistcoat and shirt—for he wore no coat—she could feel the race of his heart beating a rhythm to match hers. She started to ask what it was that he wanted to be for her, but then the front door slammed open and she sat up, and the doctor came in with Thomas and Knowles.

She had to rise, her heart still thudding and her head still spinning, and let the doctor take over. And she was left still wondering what it was that he wished he could be for her.

"Six weeks in a bloody sling! I'll give it two at the most," Ash said. He sat in his bedroom, his shirt stripped off and with Knowles rubbing something on him that smelled of turpentine and beeswax. Dr. Prichard had left it for his shoulder, and Knowles insisted on its use.

"It'll be three, and six more with you not using it for much. That's what it were last time," Knowles said.

Grumbling, Ash eased into his shirt. "I smell like a painter."

"The missus and her boys will be over this afternoon. Said she'd stop by with some of Mrs. Cranley's concoction what's supposed to be good for aching joints."

Ash thought that over for a moment and then decided that perhaps some good could come of looking romantic with his arm in a black silk sling.

Perhaps he could coax another kiss from her.

But was that wise?

That kiss had set flame to smoldering desires that in turn could lead to dangerous places. His pretty housebreaker was no worldly widow who would dally with him. No, she'd need a ring on her finger and a vow before God not to leave before she gave herself. And how could he give her such a promise?

Ah, such a pity she was so innocent.

And how he ached to bury himself in that innocence.

He let out a sigh, and Knowles cocked a knowing eyebrow.

"Oh, don't look at me like that," Ash said, slipping into a plain buff waistcoat. "I don't mean to seduce her."

"It's not her being seduced that I see," Knowles said.

Ash glowered at his servant, but the truth pulled down his shoulders like a field pack. He was being seduced. By her. By her lively boys. By the image of himself with a home and the illusion of domestic bliss.

But how long would he stay content with such simple pleasures? How long until ties to her and to this place became unbearable restrictions?

He toyed for a moment with thoughts of sweeping her off her feet, taking her away with him. He could seduce her. He knew it. He could ride off with her and her boys. They could roam together, and he would lay the world at her feet.

He went downstairs, arranging his sling and thinking of such things.

And then in the library he saw Bea nursing her kittens. Sitting down in the leather chair, he watched.

The mother cat lay contented in her cupboard, the door swung wide open to show a view of her and her kittens. When Eber tried to push Mist away, Bea reached in with a raspy tongue to wash a face and put order back into her offsprings' meal.

And Ash knew then that his dreams of taking his sweet widow away with him were all but impossible.

In truth, his pretty housebreaker shared too much in common with her cat. They were both creatures of place. Of home and habit. Pulling Emaline from this village would be as foolish as trying to pull Bea from her library. His lovely widow needed to know that she and her boys were rooted here. Oh, he might be able to coax them away, but would they thrive?

With reluctance, he thought back to his own boyhood.

He had hated being uprooted.

He had put it from his mind, from his memories, but now the uncertainty of it, the fear, the loneliness, crowded him. He liked those lads of hers far too much to put them through such an upbringing. It had left deep marks on him—in his inclination toward solitude, in his distrust of others, in his restless ways.

But if he could not stay, and she could not go, where did that leave room for anything between them?

Emaline stared at the barren trees. Winter was coming all too fast. Gray branches of the sleeping trees stretched to an even darker sky. Guy Fawkes Day had come and gone, with Knowles setting out a huge bonfire at the back of the manor. They'd had plenty to burn, and more than a few villagers came, for Sir Ashten had had the gardens cleared by them and had hired yet others to paint and to act as servants. Now the land around the house lay bare and waiting for spring's renewal.

And she had not found the courage to ask him about some sort of more binding lease. At first there had been his injured arm to think of. And then she had not wanted him to think that she had become friendly with him only to benefit herself. But she was running out of time and out of excuses to keep the inevitable at bay. She really must try to be more practical about this all.

She turned her gaze to the manor, to its lovely square form, now able to be seen. It looked like a home again, with smoke spiraling from the chimneys and lights glinting in clean windows and a new raked-gravel drive leading to the front steps.

He would be able to sell it soon for a good price.

And she dreaded the thought.

In the past few weeks the kittens had grown so that they looked more like sleek young cats, with their bodies filling out and their fur growing out from its spiky kitten-fluff. Squire Wilberforce had asked if he might take Lady Sheba Salah as a pet for his youngest daughter, and so the days were darkening in every way possible.

Soon the kittens would be gone, and so would Sir Ashten Ravenhill.

*What shall I do when he goes?*

She could not think about that. She did not want to. She tried to fool herself and tell herself that she worried only for the boys. They had become too attached to Sir Ash, as they called him. They adored that he had needed their help and had gotten so that they spent some time every day—and most evenings—up at that manor. In his company, Thomas had become more outgoing and assured. And Will followed Sir Ash about, copying his manners and his speech with an alarming likeness.

In her heart, however, she knew that she would be the one who would miss him the most.

She was not fooled into thinking that he might stay. She had spoken just yesterday with Lord Rustard, and he had mentioned again his interest in the house. The determined light in his eyes had sent a tremor of uneasiness through Emaline. Lord Rustard meant to have the manor—and he would eventually end up naming a price that Sir Ashten would accept. And then Lord Rustard would want his gate house back from her. Lease or no lease.

She really must face the inevitable.

But the shameful secret she held inside her was that she cherished a ridiculous hope that something more than flirtation had lain behind Ash's kisses.

When he had kissed her, had he longed to be a man

who could settle with her and marry? And if he wanted that, could he not become so? Was not the desire the start of all things?

Ah, but it was folly to think that way. Why would he want anything more than a kiss from a vicar's widow—a woman without beauty or money or fascinating skills? No, he had kissed her because he probably kissed any woman who would allow it. And if she tried to dream more into it than that, she would only break her own heart.

So with her head up and her armor tightened, she strode up the steps to Adair Manor.

The Findleys' eldest boy had assumed the role of footman and let her in, with a word that Knowles was in the drawing room, supervising the disassembly of the scaffolding, and Sir Ashten was in the library with the boys.

Hearing voices, she headed for the library, a smile in place.

And then she stopped in the open doorway, the sight before her freezing her step and her heart.

Sir Ashten sat in the giant leather chair, leaning forward, his injured arm pulled out from its sling as he bent over a small table. Next to the table, Thomas sat on a footstool, and Will knelt on the floor.

And both boys had cards in their hands.

Her throat dried and the bitterness surged into her like poison.

*Dear Lord, he is teaching them to gamble!*

# Eight

Fury flamed in her, burning on her face and boiling in her stomach. Her hand tightened on the doorknob, and she fought for enough control not to scream like a fishwife. My God, after all he had promised about keeping this a respectable house. She should never have trusted him. She stepped forward with the intent of carving him alive with scathing words.

And then she glimpsed his hand caress a pile of fur in his lap. The black Sir Eber and the multicolored Rue lay curled around each other. Long fingers rested protective and tender over the kittens asleep on him.

She hesitated, and then watched as Lady Mist sprawled upside down at Sir Ashten's booted feet. He reached down to scratch the kitten's gray stomach, saying to the boys as he did so, "Now feel the edge of the card for the difference between it and the one I shaved. The mark's a subtle thing, and designed so that a fellow who's had a glass too many won't notice. And that, my lads, is why a steady head in this world will serve you far better than any dependence on luck."

Her anger drained out of her, leaving her weak-limbed and shame faced. It wasn't gambling really, but a lesson how not to be taken at the tables. Suddenly, she could not help but wonder if such lessons would have kept Newell from losing the house, his fortune, and even his family's respect. What if Uncle Walter had not ranted so much about sinful ways, but had shown his son more patience and reason? Would it have made a difference?

Only if Newell had not lost the house, then Sir Ash would not have come to them.

Suddenly, she no longer knew if the man was the devil's temptation or the Lord's blessing in disguise. Perhaps he did not have to be either of those things. Perhaps it was herself who had too long viewed the world in darks and lights, in rights and wrongs. Perhaps Sir Ashten could be what he was—just another soul struggling in this world like herself.

She bit her lower lip and hung back in the doorway. The kittens, it seemed, had placed their trust in Sir Ash and looked content to keep it there. They, she knew, judged the man, not his reputation. They sensed a hand that would care for them with kindness.

Something loosened in her. Some inward constraint that had left her for too long awkward and defensive. She looked at Ash for once without seeing a gamester, and what she saw made her heart clench as if his hand had tightened over it.

For what lay before her was a man with an easy smile, a way with her children, and a heart too long dormant—just like her own. And for once it was enough to have him be so.

Straightening, she came forward into the room, asking brightly and determined to atone for her near mistake with him, "What mischief do you three plot now?"

Ash swung around, waking the kittens on his lap and frowning. Oh, damn, of all times for her to arrive. He stood, scooping up the limp kittens in his hands. Sir Eber stirred, and his eyes—which had turned from kitten blue to dark green—opened. Lazy Rea merely yawned and relaxed, as limp as if dead.

A belligerent desire to defend himself rose in Ash, and he stamped it down. He didn't need to explain himself to her and her prickly loathing of anything pleasurable. In fact, it was a good thing she'd caught him with the cards in his hands. It had been inevitable. Perhaps it was even what he had wanted when he'd suggested this diversion to the boys, for he had known in his heart that she would not approve. This way they would have a good fight about it. Then he could feel happy about taking the ten thousand that Lord Rustard had offered him, and he could quit this place without a thought.

Stiffening, he waited for the inevitable hot contempt from her for his sinful ways.

She smiled up at him, then tousled Thomas's hair and bent over the makeshift card table. "Who is winning?"

"We're not playing, Mother," Thomas said, his tone scornful, as if she had not seen the obvious.

"Sir Ash is showing us how to avoid Captain Sharps," Will added.

"Well, perhaps he can also show you a little bit of whist as well. It has been, oh, since well before I married that I last played, but I used to like it quite well. Your grandmother and I used to play for the meringues that Cook made, so perhaps Mrs. Crawley will make some for us."

"Meringues!" Will jumped up at the mention of his favorite treat of baked sugar and egg whites. "Can I ask her now?"

"You may," she said, and the boys thundered out with only a last-minute-remembered polite bow.

Ash watched this, uneasy and still braced for war. What was her game? Had she not wanted to trim him down before the boys? His tone hostile, he asked, "Well?"

She smiled again, a little hesitant, then reached out

to stroke Sir Eber's black head, her hand coming so close to his that it distracted him.

"Your arm seems better," she said.

Realizing that he had pulled off his sling, he glanced down. He gestured with the near-comatose Reu to a chair, and when Emaline sat, he also sat down, settling the kittens back to their napping locations. Lady Mist jumped up onto Emaline's lap and Ash watched her stroke the kitten, thinking all the time—*lucky cat.*

"Aren't you going to say something?" he blurted out, unable to bear the waiting.

She dimpled. "About your arm? Or about the cards?"

"The dam—dashed cards. I know you despise them. . . ." *And me as well for being so impossibly linked to them.*

She hesitated a moment, glancing down to the gray kitten in her lap and seeming to choose her words with care. "*Despise* is a rather strong word. And while I may despise what they did to my cousin—or, rather, what he did with them, I fear that perhaps I have been as wrong in my condemnation of them. Does not the Bible tell us that it is those without sin who should cast the first stone at another? And self-righteousness is such an awful sin."

Deliberate and provoking, he said, "I wouldn't know about that. I haven't read a Bible in years."

And still she smiled at him, as indulgent as if she were dealing with Will, not a man grown.

"Then I shall take Bea and her kittens for my examples, for you do know them, and they offer nothing but love to those who care for them." She ducked her head low, seemingly to pet Bea, who had come out of the cupboard with her other two kittens. With the slightest tremor in her voice, she added, "Do you not think that is a good example to follow?"

He sat here, numb, his throat dry and wondering

why she was doing this to him. She could not possibly be hinting at what he thought she was with this talk of love. Not with him. His voice harsh and low, he asked, "What do you want from me?"

She put down Lady Mist and rose, and came over to stand before him. He started to rise, but she lay a white, slim hand on his shoulder, and it stayed him as if she had tied him with weights. "Do not disturb the kittens again. They look so comfortable. And there is but one thing you can do for me—just be happy, Ash. You are a gentleman who deserves that and far more, you know."

Leaning down, she kissed his cheek, a flutter of softness against his face, and then in a swish of skirts she was gone, slipped away like a dream of springtime.

He sat for a very long time, slowly stroking Eber's soft fur and scratching behind Reu's left ear, and thinking about his life, about her, and about too many other things.

Emaline had to come back the next day to collect Lady Mist for Squire Wilberforce. The kittens were old enough now to head to new homes, and it was best that they go before they began to think the manor their lifelong residence. They would most likely take after Bea in their attachment to place.

*Just like me,* she thought as she walked through the bare beech woods.

And then she wondered if she would go with him if he asked.

She looked around her, seeing a winter-bleak world ready for snow and rain. It seemed that as a woman she was making up for not having been a foolish girl. She had fallen in love with a man she could not have, and her heart both ached and soared. How was it possible to feel both the thrill of love and its heartache?

But she did. And she feared that if he did ask, she would say yes. Could she do that to the boys? Could she uproot them for a wandering existence?

The only answer that came to mind was that her heart would bleed if he left without her. And so would the boys'.

A few last leaves still clung to the trees, tenuous and determined to hang on. Am I like that? Clinging to place when I ought to let go and let God guide me to what is next? And then she looked to the trees. If she left, how she would miss seeing them leaf out in the spring. And she would miss Mrs. Crawley, and what would she do with Bea? She had so many deep roots here.

She paused at the turn that led up to the manor.

A carriage stood in the drive, blankets laid over the horses to keep them warm against the bite of winter that lay in the wind. Pulling her cloak closer, as if it would hide her, Emaline watched as Lord Rustard and Sir Ashten came out of the house. They paused on the steps to shake hands, Lord Rustard smiling with smug satisfaction. He got into his carriage, grooms hurried to pull off the horse blankets, and then the carriage moved off, clattering past where she stood, hidden by the trees.

When she looked back to the steps, Ash had gone.

*So it is done. He has sold.*

With her heart beating fast in her throat, she started toward the house again, half dreading that he would ask her to go with him, and praying that he would not so that she would not have to decide.

Ash stood in the library, dangling a ribbon for the kittens to chase. They were still kitten enough to be easily lured into mock chases, and they pounced the ribbon—and one another—with more comic clumsiness than skilled grace. Bea lay nearby, cleaning her coat and keeping an eye on the games.

Ash laughed aloud as Sir Eber caught the ribbon

and then had to let it go as the marmalade Lady Sheba Salah pounced him, igniting a battle.

And then some instinct made him turn to the door.

She stood there much as he had first seen her, tousled and with that wretched cloak hiding most of her from his view. He gave up the ribbons to the kittens and moved to her.

"If I had an ounce of wisdom, I should have tossed that cloak of yours onto the Guy Fawkes bonfire."

She put up a protective hand to the ties. "My cloak? I will have you know this is fine Shropshire wool and has seen me good service."

"Too much service." He took it from her and tossed it aside and then led her toward the chairs by the fire. The kittens chased after the flung-aside cloak and started a game of hide-and-seek beneath its folds.

"You see," he said, "Bea's kittens know a better use for that antique of yours."

She had to smile as Sir Eber poked his head out, only to have it slapped by Lady Mist. Then she glanced up at Ash, her expression sobering. "I saw Lord Rustard leaving. I beg your pardon for asking, but since it rather affects me, I would like to know if you have reached an agreement with him on a sale?"

Ash frowned. He rose from his chair and went to stand by the fireplace. Not knowing what to do with his hands, he shoved them into his breeches, and then he pulled one out again to drag through his hair. Damn, how did he put this? The words he had rehearsed all night in his mind suddenly stuck in his throat.

What would she say to his offer? What if this were a dreadful mistake?

He turned and picked up the poker to jab at an already burning fire. The movement gave him an instant to pull together his courage.

When he turned back, he saw a streaking black form chased by an orange one dart under Emaline's skirts.

The kittens distracted her, bringing laughter to those tawny eyes, and he knew then this was no mistake. It would never be one so long as he could see those sherry eyes lighten with delight. He knew the name for the desire, the longing, that had driven him home to England. But could he have what he wanted? He certainly did not deserve it.

"Emaline?" he said, and she turned her gaze on him, her glance full of the longing that lay in his own heart.

He was across the distance between them in an instant and had her in his arms as she rose up to him. Her mouth met his with the same urgent desire, the same hot need, the same trembling uncertainty. And then he lost track of all else.

Until sharp claws slapped at his boot and a small furry body careened between his legs.

Pulling back, he looked down at Emaline's face. Her golden lashes slowly pulled open, and he stared at her, searching her expression for the certainty of her heart.

"Take me with you," she whispered.

He shook his head. "The boys need a home. And you . . . you, my pretty housebreaker, are as married to this house, this land, as your precious Begat, and as her kittens after her shall be."

Her eyes filmed with tears, but a small frown tightened on her brow. "Her kittens?"

His arms tightened around her. "Yes. And her kitten's kittens. And the kittens that come after that. I'm afraid I'm tangled in a cat's cradle here."

"But Lord Rustard . . . ?"

"Bought some of my property by the river and two tenant farms. I haven't the funds to mend them as they need, but he does, and he was quite satisfied that he is now the largest property holder in the county. He also seemed pleased to take me under his wing with advice. I think he has ambitions to see me made over into a gentleman farmer, and he likes the notion that he shall be viewed as the mentor who reformed me. Of course, we'll know that's not true."

She stared up at him, her expression confused. "You're staying? You will not tire of this place?"

He smoothed the trouble from her face. "Tire of it? I think that you—yes, and those imps you call sons—are what I've been searching for my whole life. I'm home, my sweet Em. That is, I am if you say I am. For it all rests in your hands now."

He took her hands and kissed each palm. And then she pulled them away from her to wrap her arms tight around his neck.

"You are always home in my arms," she whispered to him, and delight swirled in her as his lips claimed hers again.

And from beside the hearth, Bea watched, indulgently, her tail twitching as her kittens romped around the entwined forms, smug in her sense of home and place.

# Lord Wintergreen and the Beast

Mona Gedney

Lord Wintergreen had little patience with his fellow man, so when a beggar pressed too close to him as he prepared to cross the busy street, he felt no compunction about pushing the man to one side. He had no desire to be troubled by such riffraff. Nor did he pay any particular attention to the problem that his action caused, for the beggar stumbled into an elderly woman in the crowd, sending her tumbling to the pavement, her basket of goods scattering among the boots and slippers of passersby.

"Here, sir! Come back and help this woman that you overset!"

Wintergreen heard the imperious command and felt a sharp tug at his elbow. Not being accustomed to such treatment, he turned in amazement and stared at the speaker. A young woman was bending over the older one, helping her to her feet and straightening her worn cloak and dark bonnet for her.

"Do you not see the trouble you have caused her?" the young woman continued, giving her attention to the victim and not sparing a glance for him. "There is her shopping being trodden upon by passersby, and no one can be bothered to help her—including the one who is responsible for her fall."

"You appear to be doing that for all of us," remarked Wintergreen coolly.

"Thank you, miss," said the old woman, looking at him nervously. She recognized a member of the quality when she saw one, and his disdainful expression told her in an instant that he had no wish to be troubled by her problems. "Don't you worry about my bits and pieces."

"Nonsense," replied her rescuer crisply, snatching up a loaf of bread before a passing horseman rode over it. She looked down at it in disgust, for its golden crust was already dusty.

She motioned toward Wintergreen, saying to the old woman, "Since your goods have been damaged, I am certain that this gentleman will wish to apologize and to replace the things that you have lost because of his carelessness."

Wintergreen, who was never spoken to in such a manner, stared at her without saying a word. Whether he was more astonished by her behavior or her appearance was not at all clear to him. She was a striking woman, perhaps a beautiful one, but even beautiful women of high station treated him with deference because of his rank, fortune, and personal attributes.

The young woman before him clearly felt no such deference. Although her voice was controlled, her eyes were stormy, and she looked at him as though she had discovered something particularly distasteful after turning over a rock.

When he did not respond, she opened her own reticule and began counting out coins into the old woman's palm. "Here you are, ma'am," she said, not bothering to look at Wintergreen again. "Do be careful in the crowds, for you can see that even gentlemen—perhaps especially gentlemen—will have little regard for your sex or your age."

"Thank you, miss," said the old woman, bobbing her head and disappearing into the throng, eager to put some distance between herself and the forbidding gentleman who was scowling at them. The young woman watched her to be certain that she was all right, then hurried across the street herself, never looking at Wintergreen again and certainly not troubled by his disapproval.

All of this had happened very rapidly, and Wintergreen found himself following her, overtaking her as she was about to enter a bookshop.

Taking a sovereign from his pocket, he handed it to her. "I have no wish for someone else to pay my debts—or, I should say, what are incorrectly perceived to be my debts," he said stiffly.

She looked at the sovereign, then at him. "I do not accept money from strangers, sir," she said, her tone well bred and distant. "It was to the woman you wronged that you owed your money—and your assistance."

She turned away and entered the bookshop, closing the door sharply behind her.

Wintergreen stood there a moment, looking after her, his cheeks flushed at her effrontery. She was wrong, of course. The beggar had knocked over the old woman; *he* had not done so. He could not be expected to answer for the consequences of each movement he made.

Still, he was a man accustomed to respect, and he was unpleasantly aware that the young woman in the bookshop regarded him with undisguised disdain. It did not matter, of course, but it was mildly troubling that she should have so misguided a view of him. And if she went around giving away her shillings to strangers, she would soon be without, for he had seen at a glance that her attire, although in simple good taste, was not the clothing of a woman of means.

He watched through the bookshop window until she glanced up, caught his eye, then firmly turned her back upon him. Irritated, he turned toward home. There, at least, he would have some peace.

He soon discovered, however, that peace was not to

be had. When the butler opened the door and ushered him in, he informed Wintergreen that Albert Sperling, who handled his business affairs, was awaiting him in the library. A few words from that gentleman were all that was required to complete the ruin of his afternoon.

"What do you mean, she can't be bought off? Good Lord, Sperling! Five thousand pounds is enough for some wench at a country inn!"

Sperling shuffled nervously in the face of his employer's wrath. Lord Wintergreen was never a mild-mannered man at the best of times, and this was very far from the best of times. Avoiding Wintergreen's piercing gaze, he murmured uneasily, "She doesn't want money, my lord."

He waited for a moment and then added reluctantly, "And forgive me for saying so, but I don't believe she could be called a wench. She seems to be a young woman of some breeding."

Wintergreen glared at him. "And why would a young lady of breeding be running an inn?" he demanded. "Or sending me letters that hint at blackmail?" He paused a moment and waited for a reply. "Isn't that exactly what she has done?"

Sperling nodded uncomfortably. "As I said, her second letter states that she does not want money, but I am afraid, my lord, that she might make life most unpleasant for you if you don't provide what she does want."

"The devil you say! What does she think she can possibly do to me? And what *does* she want?"

Sperling closed his eyes, knowing what was to come. "I fear, my lord, that the lady says she will make her son's identity publicly known—and say that you refuse to recognize him officially because you do not wish to lose your title."

He shuddered as a vase shattered against the wall behind his head, and kept his eyes tightly closed as

Wintergreen disposed of two or three other breakable pieces. When things grew quiet, he opened his eyes carefully. To his relief, his employer had sunk into an armchair by the hearth and was staring into the fire.

"What a woman like that says will make no difference! I won't recognize him!" Wintergreen said bitterly, although his voice was lower now. "My brother has been dead these ten years, and now she suddenly appears and wants to blacken his name. I won't have it!"

Sperling inched a little closer. "Perhaps you should go to this inn—to the Golden Lion—and inspect them yourself, my lord."

Noting the flash in Lord Wintergreen's eyes, he added hurriedly, "You need not make yourself known, of course. You could stop as a chance traveler, as I did. After observing the boy and his mother, you could then determine what steps you wish to take."

Sperling waited a minute or two, bracing himself for another bout of china shattering, but there was no response. Wintergreen remained oblivious to him, staring into the fire without speaking another word. Finally, Sperling bowed and murmured his farewell, closing the door quietly behind him.

A full two hours later, the butler entered quietly and built up the fire, but a glance at his master's face invited no question about further orders. Accustomed to Wintergreen's ways, he remained silent and satisfied himself with placing a bottle of brandy and a glass on a tray at his master's elbow, then removed himself without a sound.

As Lord Wintergreen stared unseeingly at the flickering flames, he did not at first think about the news that Sperling had brought him; instead, he thought of his childhood and of Edward, gone these ten years. It did not seem as though it could be so. Edward had been so vibrantly alive, his dark eyes alight with curiosity and mischief and—whenever they had turned to his younger brother—affection. He had driven the butler wild by dismantling the grandfather clock so that he could see how it worked, then shocked everyone by putting it back in working order again. Without permission, he had taken his father's prize hunter out and ridden him over the roughest terrain in the county, returning both the hunter and himself intact to a wild-eyed groom.

No matter what mischief he made, however, he had been instantly forgiven because of his endearing manner. The only one in whom he had failed to inspire affection was their cold and distant father. Their mother had died long ago, and her sons had been reared by a succession of nannies and tutors, then sent away to boarding school at the first possible moment.

Five years had separated them. Once Edward had left Oxford, he had antagonized their father by protesting the treatment of the tenants of their several estates, demanding that their rents be lowered and their cottages kept in better repair. Their father, weary of his son's criticism and eager for a little peace, had sent him to inspect the family holdings in the other hemisphere, a plantation in Barbados and another not far from New Orleans.

For a brief moment, Wintergreen wondered uncomfortably what Edward would have said of his behavior in the encounter with the old woman and her defender today, but he promptly dismissed the thought as a matter of little consequence, and he turned again to the past.

He smiled as he remembered how jealous he had been of his brother's adventure. He himself had been wild to join the cavalry, but their father had informed him that his heir—even though he was second in line instead of first—would be doing nothing so dangerous, that he would do as he was told and complete his education at Oxford. Instead of returning obediently to school, however, he had joined the army and, at nineteen, gone to fight in the Peninsular War.

It was just a year later when he had received a letter from his father, announcing tersely that Edward had died of malaria in New Orleans. It was only to be expected, the letter had continued, for Edward had written to him earlier, renouncing his title and declaring his intention of remaining in New Orleans to take up life with heaven only knew what riffraff.

"I was certain that he would not last long once he no longer received his quarterly allowance," their father had written, "so I cut him off immediately. In time, he would have realized that he had made a grievous error and resumed his proper place. After all, at home he had waiting a position of power and a beautiful young woman to whom he was betrothed. Now that Edward is gone and you are my heir, I shall naturally expect you to resign your commission and come home immediately."

Wintergreen had read that letter beside a campfire in the mountains of Spain, surrounded by the familiar laughter of his comrades and the rich fragrance of wood smoke and coffee. Regardless of the company, a wave of desolation had washed over him, a loneliness that had left him almost breathless.

"What is it, Trev?" one of his companions had asked him. "Bad news from home?"

He hadn't answered, rising abruptly and striding into the shadows so that he could be alone with his pain. And now he was truly alone, he had told himself, unable to believe that Edward, so bright-eyed and vibrant with life, the only person he loved and who had loved him in return, was gone. It seemed to him that those he loved always left him—his laughing, bright-eyed mother had died when he was three, leaving them to their father's cold care. During his childhood, even the nanny to whom he had grown attached had been removed from him, for his father did not believe in encouraging emotional dependence upon anyone. And now Edward was gone.

Accepting the news of the death of his father, which arrived some six months later, had been far less difficult. After learning of Edward's death, he had written immediately to his father, informing him that he planned to remain with his regiment and would not be returning to England for some time. The flagrant disobedience of his two sons had apparently had a detrimental effect upon Lord Wintergreen, or perhaps sixty years of indulgent living had simply caught up with him. In any case, he had collapsed and died shortly after receiving Trevor's letter. Feeling some guilt over the death of his father, he had gone home to accept his responsibilities as the new Earl of Wintergreen.

The fire had again grown low before Lord Wintergreen emerged from his reverie, but he had by then determined his course of action. To Sperling's infinite relief, he decided to journey alone to the Golden Lion and to see for himself what problem Marguerite Stanwick and her son presented. Sperling had no taste for confrontation, and he could only imagine what Wintergreen might do when he came face to face with a woman he considered no better than a thief.

He had no very high opinion of people in general, and, having been the quarry of many a fortune-hunting young woman, the earl's view of the fair sex was particularly low. This woman's behavior had served only to confirm his belief that people were self-centered and rapacious and completely untrustworthy.

The next day the earl drove from London at a brisk clip, determined to put an end to the ridiculous demands of Marguerite Stanwick. The beauties of the autumn countryside were lost upon him, for he concentrated studiously upon what he would say to her once he had taken her measure. He planned to stay at the inn as an ordinary traveler, reconnoiter, and then inform her of his identity and his assessment of her character.

When Wintergreen arrived at the Golden Lion, he handed the ribbons of his racing curricle carelessly to an ostler, who took them reverently, overcome by the elegance of both driver and vehicle, as well as the peerless quality of the pair of bays. Wintergreen's attention was entirely upon the inn itself, a comfortable-looking establishment of rosy brick, its windows bright in the frosty twilight.

He had decided to travel alone. He did not wish for anyone in his own household to know about this problem from Edward's past, nor did he wish for either his valet or groom to say anything that would betray his real identity. He was traveling as Mr. James Harding, Esquire, so that he could inspect his quarry without arousing suspicion.

Entering the taproom, he looked around him with unwilling approval. Everything was neatly kept and freshly polished, the ancient wooden counter of the bar glowing in the light of the crackling fire. The man behind it served him cheerfully, and when he inquired whether there was a room available for the night, the waiter nodded, announcing that he would tell Mrs. Stanwick that they had a guest.

Wintergreen's lips tightened, deeply resenting the fact that the woman was using his family name. He supposed he should be grateful that she had not styled herself the Dowager Countess of Wintergreen. The letter he had received from her had announced that Edward had married her in New Orleans and that she had borne him a son after his death. It had also informed him that she lived now in England, where she kept a country inn.

Since Wintergreen had considered the letter no more than a thinly disguised attempt to extort money from him, he had had Sperling reply to it, reluctant even to read it all the way through himself. Wintergreen was not inclined to fret over a threat to his title. Chiefly, he resented the shadow cast upon his brother's memory.

He had not been surprised to learn from his father that Edward had given up his title and decided to begin a new life in a new world. He had had no love for society life, nor for the lady to whom their father had betrothed him, and he had been wild for adventure. Nonetheless, Wintergreen was certain that Edward would have informed them had he decided to marry, and no such letter had ever arrived.

A movement beside him drew his attention from his tankard of ale, whose depths he had been studying for some minutes.

"I understand you wish a room for the night, sir."

The voice was low and musical, and its owner the striking young woman he had encountered on the street in London.

"You are Mrs. Stanwick?" he asked in disbelief.

She nodded calmly. "Just which part of that surprises you, sir? My name or the fact that I keep an inn?"

Thoroughly annoyed with himself for being caught off guard, he answered carefully. "Both, I must confess," he replied. "I had thought you too young to be a married woman, and too well-bred—"

He paused a moment to choose his words. He had no intention of offending her before he had had an opportunity to observe her closely.

She regarded him with amusement. "Certainly you did not think me too well-bred to be an innkeeper. More like you thought that I was a fishwife. I believe that my manner offended you."

"The incident was an unfortunate one," Wintergreen said. "I fear that it did neither of us credit."

"Certainly it did you none," she agreed, "and I don't believe that you appreciated my frankness."

"Perhaps not at the time," he responded, disliking himself for his duplicity, for he did not like her honesty then or now, "but after thinking it over, I realized that I had acted in haste." He had thought no such thing, nor did he think it now, but he did wish to placate her. He could hope to discover nothing about her if she held him in dislike.

"Did you indeed?" Mrs. Stanwick asked in surprise, her brows lifted. She obviously did not think him capable of changing his mind and feeling regret over an error, and Wintergreen was unaccountably irritated with her attitude, even though she was, of course, correct.

He allowed himself to study her for a moment, and he was pleased with what he saw. Her strong features were delicately chiseled, her dark hair smoothly coiled at the base of her neck. Her most arresting quality, however, was her eyes. They were, he thought before he could catch himself, as changeable as the sea, a curious mixture of gray and green and blue, and their expression was decidedly intelligent and alert. Just now they were distant and a little watchful, the cool gray prevailing, but he remembered that the green had predominated in their angry encounter on the street.

Despite his prejudice against her, both because of her letters and because of their first meeting, he found himself thinking that he would not be amazed if his brother had indeed loved such a woman. She was as different from the Dresden china doll to whom Edward had been engaged as it was possible to be.

Surprised and displeased by his unaccustomed susceptibility to a pretty face, he promptly stifled the thought, nodding to her coolly. "I did, ma'am."

She appeared to consider this for a moment, then nodded as though she had made up her mind.

"Then, if you will be so good as to come with me,

I will show you to your chamber." She bent to pick up the valise standing beside him, but he retrieved it first and followed her from the taproom. Her gown was the color of evergreens, and he noticed with annoyance that she moved gracefully as she climbed the narrow stairs that led to his room.

He deposited the valise just inside the small chamber to which to she led him, then turned and hurried after her, for she made no effort to show him his room or to prolong the conversation. Whatever she might be, he thought, Marguerite Stanwick was at least no common flirt, which was a part of the picture he had painted for himself after receiving her letters.

"This is a pleasing establishment, Mrs. Stanwick," he observed to her back as they made their way downstairs again.

"I'm glad that you think so, Mr. Harding," she replied, her manner inviting no further conversation.

Finding himself dismissed, Wintergreen returned to the taproom to make himself comfortable and to observe what he could during the course of the evening. He maintained his place at his table for some time, watching the local citizenry come and go. Despite himself, he was forced to admit that the inn appeared to be competently run and the customers, although rustic, civil enough in manner.

Mrs. Stanwick appeared once, and then only to step into the room and survey the scene, smiling to the men, who turned to speak to her or even, Wintergreen noted in astonishment, to pull an occasional forelock in a gesture of respect. He had not seen such old-fashioned deference since he was a boy. He waited for her to speak to him, but she did not acknowledge his presence.

Finally, after a satisfying dinner of toad-in-the-hole, a dish that hearkened back to his nursery days, Wintergreen retired to his room. Once again, almost against his will, he was impressed by its pleasant comfort, and he fell asleep on lavender-scented sheets, as he had in his childhood.

His awakening was a little less peaceful. A sudden weight dropped on his chest, and he heard a young voice say sharply, "For shame, Beast! He's a guest! You mustn't do that, you know."

Wintergreen attempted to open his eyes and focus on the owner of the voice. He could see at first only a blurred figure, and he was still keenly aware of the sudden weight.

"I am sorry, sir," the voice added apologetically. "That's why we call him the Beast, you know. He sneaks up on his prey—usually one of us—and then he pounces."

Wintergreen stared at the marmalade-colored cat on his chest, who returned the gaze with equal intensity. Then he looked at the boy who had been speaking, and he felt a knot in his throat.

This was Edward's child, of that he was certain. Everything about him spoke of Edward—the dark, curly hair, the high cheekbones, the slender form—everything about him but the eyes, which were the same color as his mother's. But even the eyes, he noted, were as earnest and intense as Edward's had been.

"What is your name, boy?" he had demanded, speaking more sharply than he had intended.

"Grant Stanwick, sir," he had replied, turning pink at Wintergreen's tone. "My mother is mistress of this inn." He scooped Beast from Wintergreen's bed and glared at the cat. "And I apologize again, sir, for the fright that Beast gave you."

Wintergreen managed a smile. "I think that I will recover," he assured the boy, and was rewarded with a smile.

"Thank you, sir," he said gratefully. "I'll try to see to it that Beast doesn't bother you again."

Wintergreen stared dubiously at Beast, who studied

him with an unblinking golden gaze as Grant draped the cat over his shoulder and let himself out of the room. Grant might be determined to keep Beast away, but Wintergreen was less certain that the cat himself would be deterred by any such intentions.

As he prepared to go down to breakfast, he arranged the crisp white folds of his cravat with deft fingers, still thinking about the child whom he had just met. He would have to be provided for, of course. He could not do less for Edward's son. He was certain, however, that Edward had not married the boy's mother—not without notifying his brother of such a momentous step or taking the proper measures to protect any children of the marriage. And to think that Edward would have married a woman who would be mistress of an inn was beyond imagination. He had been betrothed to Belinda Malston, the only child of a marquis, a woman of wealth, beauty, and position. Lovely though Marguerite Stanwick might be, she could scarcely compete with such attractions.

Turning from his looking glass to the window, he saw with pleasure that dark clouds scudded across the skies and rain was beginning to pelt the panes. This turn in the weather would offer him a perfect excuse for lingering at the inn and studying the boy and his mother.

With that end in mind, he took up residence at a table by the fire in the taproom, ordering a hearty breakfast of beefsteaks and ale.

"How long have you been at the Golden Lion?" he asked the white-haired waiter who had served him the night before.

"Thirty years, sir," he replied.

"Not all that time with Mrs. Stanwick, surely," he said lightly, hoping that the man would be talkative.

The waiter smiled broadly. "Oh, no, sir. As I'm certain you've noticed, she is too young for that. Mrs.

Stanwick has been here only the past two years. Before that I served Mr. Comstock."

"Indeed?" returned Wintergreen a little absently. So she had been here for two years. Why, he wondered, had it taken her so long to mail her first letter to him? And what had brought her to this particular inn?

"Was she a relative of Mr. Comstock's?" he asked.

The waiter shook his head, busily polishing a brass andiron. "Her father had helped Mr. Comstock when he was just a boy, and Mr. Comstock never forgot it. When he had no family of his own and he knew he was dying, he wrote to Mrs. Stanwick's father and told him that he was leaving the Lion to him. When Mrs. Stanwick's father died before he could come here, the solicitor told her that since she was her father's heir, the Golden Lion was hers. She was free to sell it or to come here and run it."

"And are you glad she came here instead of selling it?" inquired Wintergreen curiously.

"Indeed I am, sir," he answered seriously, polishing the glasses before him intently. "Mrs. Stanwick takes good care of us. Not one of the six of us who worked for Mr. Comstock was let go, not even Joseph, who is past the age for working in the stables. She wrote to the solicitor that no one was to lose his job. Joseph was told to oversee the care of the horses and vehicles and the stable hands so that he didn't have to do the hard work anymore."

The man grinned. "Joseph has been lording it over the two stable boys ever since. Their lives haven't been worth living."

Wintergreen didn't reply, and the waiter polished with still greater intensity and his eyes grew brighter. "It were a kind thing to do, as you can see, sir—but it's no more than you'd expect from a pastor's daughter."

"A pastor's daughter?" asked Wintergreen, startled.

"Do you mean to say that Mrs. Stanwick's father was a man of the cloth?"

The waiter nodded. "As I told you, he were the one that helped Mr. Comstock long ago."

"Good morning, Mr. Harding."

To his surprise, he discovered Mrs. Stanwick standing at his elbow. Aware that she must have heard his question, he suddenly felt oddly ill at ease, as though he had been caught in what she would consider yet another lapse of manners. He stood and pulled out a chair for her, which she ignored.

"I must apologize to you for my son's cat," she continued, studying him quite frankly. "I am afraid that being awakened in such a manner must have been decidedly unpleasant."

The waiter chuckled. "Beast pounced upon you, did he, sir?"

Wintergreen nodded. "Does he awaken all your guests in that charming manner?" he inquired.

Marguerite Stanwick smiled for the first time and shook her head. "Fortunately, no, or we would not have enough guests to earn our bread and butter. You must have been of particular interest to him."

"I am honored," he replied gravely. "And I hope to give him the opportunity to inspect me again. I'm afraid I'm not equipped for traveling in hard weather such as this, and I would like to stay on another night if I may keep my room."

The rain was now coming down steadily.

"Of course," she said. Seeing the waiter approach with Wintergreen's breakfast, she added, "Grainger, do not allow Mr. Harding to pay for his breakfast. I think that is the least we may do for him after Beast's attack."

Before Wintergreen could protest, she had turned toward the door, for Grant had entered, followed closely by Beast, who, seeing Wintergreen, had hurried over and was rubbing langorously against his boots.

"Here now! Come away, Beast! You've done enough for one morning!" the boy scolded, snatching up his cat, who eyed all of them, unperturbed.

"Mr. Channing will be here soon, Grant. You'd best take Beast and go prepare for your lessons," said his mother, smiling at her son and ruffling his hair.

Grant bowed briefly to Wintergreen and moved slowly to the door. "I'd like to see your bays, sir. Will you be leaving soon?"

Amused, Wintergreen shook his head. He could almost see Edward before him, eager to be off to the stables. "I plan to stay a bit longer because of the weather. There will be time enough for you to see them."

"Thank you, sir," replied the boy gratefully, and he hurried from the room.

"That was kind of you, Mr. Harding, but quite unnecessary," observed his mother. "Grant has always been mad for horses, but he needs to be equally mad for his lessons."

"Is Mr. Channing his tutor?" inquired Wintergreen curiously. He was resolved to discover as much as possible about Edward's son so that he could determine what should be done for him. As for what was to be done about his mother's pretensions, he was less certain now, but that could be decided at his leisure.

Mrs. Stanwick nodded. "Mr. Channing is our vicar, and he has taken a great interest in Grant's education. We are most fortunate."

Wintergreen wondered briefly about Mr. Channing's motive for taking such an interest in the son of an innkeeper, but he was not left long in doubt. The door opened and a dark young man, soberly attired, entered.

"Mrs. Stanwick," he said, bowing low and taking her hand. So absorbed was he that it took a moment for him to realize there was someone else with her.

Mrs. Stanwick introduced them, and the gentlemen made their bows. Wintergreen noticed with some amusement that Mr. Channing took on a striking resemblance to a stiff-legged terrier guarding his bone. Mrs. Stanwick was clearly the bone.

"Grant is waiting for you in the book room, Mr. Channing," she said, leading him from the taproom. Channing cast one baleful glance toward Wintergreen as he turned, then smiled down at the lady and followed in her wake.

"How often does the boy receive his lessons?" Wintergreen inquired casually of Grainger.

"As often as the vicar can manage to come," observed the waiter dryly. "If he had his way, he'd be here every day and twice on Sundays."

"Enjoys his tutoring, does he?" asked Wintergreen.

"Enjoys Mrs. Stanwick," replied Grainger, "although it's not my place to say so. He likes the boy well enough, but he'd be happier if he could arrange to have her in the room with them for the whole time he's here. After the boy's lessons, the vicar hangs about like a puppy when she's trying to work or when she's just wishful of a bit of time for herself."

A pair of customers entered the taproom just then, and Grainger went to serve them. Clearly, their chat was over for the moment.

Wintergreen situated himself comfortably on the settle in front of the fire and decided to bide his time. Unquestionably, the lady would reappear at some point, and he could engage her in conversation again. She seemed to be making an effort to do well by her son, but he was determined to know more about them both.

He sat with his legs comfortably crossed, his feet close to the fire, but he did not sit alone for long. A throaty purr alerted him to the arrival of Beast, who was comfortably ensconced just under his legs. There appeared to be no escape from the cat, he reflected.

He was not fond of cats, but he could see that if he wished to ingratiate himself with the boy and his mother, he would have to tolerate this one.

"Comfortable?" he inquired dryly, looking down at the cat.

Beast opened one golden eye, stared at him for a moment, then closed it and resumed his purring. Wintergreen shut his eyes, and the two of them dozed quietly before the fire.

"I see that you've been adopted," observed Mrs. Stanwick a few minutes later, appearing noiselessly at his side.

Sitting up abruptly, Wintergreen startled Beast, who stared at him reproachfully, stretched, and then took himself away, the picture of injured dignity.

"Yes, I see that I've been singled out," he replied, his tone indicating that he was not particularly struck by the honor.

"This is unusual behavior for Beast," said his hostess thoughtfully. "It must be that you particularly dislike cats, and he can sense it."

Somewhat ruffled by this accurate assessment, Wintergreen denied it firmly. "There have always been cats in my household," he replied. He did not think it necessary to add that they were always confined to the stable area and never allowed the run of the house.

"We have always had cats too," said Mrs. Stanwick. "Grant is especially fond of Beast though. He has been a pet since we first came to the Golden Lion."

"And when was that?" asked Wintergreen. Seeing her surprise at his interest, he added hurriedly, "Has Beast been the boy's pet for a long time?"

Reassured that his interest was in Grant and the cat, she nodded. "We have been here for two years."

"The cat didn't move here with you?" he asked casually.

"No, I don't think Beast would have cared for the

journey over on the ship," she said, smiling at the thought.

"Then you came from out of the country?" he said, feigning surprise.

She nodded again, and he found himself thinking that she was a singularly beautiful woman, all the more so because she seemed completely unaware of it.

"We sailed from Boston," she replied. "My father was a minister there, and we made our home with him. But then," she added, looking at him frankly, "you already know a part of that, for I heard Grainger telling you."

Wintergreen smiled easily. "Yes, I must apologize for my curiosity, but it seemed odd to me for a woman so obviously well-bred to be keeping an inn."

"Yes, I'm certain that your first impression of me was that I was a woman of good breeding," she observed mildly, her lips curved in the hint of a smile, as though she were mocking both of them. "I wasn't certain just how it would be here, but it has worked out quite well. Grant is happy enough, and I keep busy with the inn."

"Have you no other family?" he asked, watching her carefully.

There was a perceptible pause, and he thought she colored slightly, but there was no other sign of subterfuge. "No," she replied briefly. "We are quite alone."

"Now," she added, rising and obviously intent upon putting a period to the conversation, "I must see to it that Mary is at work, or we shall have to do without our dinner."

"A serious matter," he agreed, rising to bow to her as she left the room. As he turned back to the fire, Beast sprang from the settle and attached himself to Wintergreen's right top-boot so that he appeared to be hugging it.

Wintergreen regarded him thoughtfully for a moment, fighting back his inclination to shake the animal off. Instead, he reached down and carefully detached Beast, one paw at a time, leaving behind a trail of claw marks. His valet, who took great pride in sending his master out into the world immaculately attired, would be distraught by the damage.

"It is just as well that Appelby cannot see this, Beast," Wintergreen remarked reflectively. "You would be in imminent danger if he could."

"Beast!" exclaimed Grant, appearing suddenly beside them. "What have you done?" The boy flushed and turned to Wintergreen. "I'm very sorry he is behaving so poorly, Mr. Harding. I can't think why he has singled you out."

"Your mother has a theory," replied Wintergreen as he looked at the cat's steady golden gaze, "and I believe she may be quite correct. But you mustn't take it so much to heart," he added kindly, seeing the boy's stricken expression.

"I'll polish them for you, sir," said Grant, studying Wintergreen's boots anxiously.

"Nonsense!" returned Wintergreen, touched by his concern. "I daresay Beast would take that as an invitation to attack once more, so I think we'd best leave them as they are."

Grant reluctantly allowed himself to be convinced, and accepted Wintergreen's invitation to sit down and talk with him awhile.

"I hadn't expected to be here longer than overnight," he remarked disingenuously, "so I would enjoy a little company to pass the time. How was your lesson with your tutor?"

"Just as it always is," Grant replied, then colored to his hairline. "I beg your pardon, sir. That sounds ungrateful to Mr. Channing and rude to you. It's just that—"

"Just that you don't care for your Latin?" said Wintergreen helpfully. "I never cared for it myself."

Grant smiled gratefully. "No, I don't like it very well, sir, but I try to do my best. I'd rather be out riding or helping my mother with the inn."

Wintergreen smiled to himself. Horses again; the boy was Edward to the core. "I always felt the same myself—about horses, that is. My mother died when I was young."

"I'm sorry to hear it, sir," Grant said politely. After a moment of reflection, he added, "My father died before I was born."

"Did he, indeed?" asked Wintergreen, his heart quickening. This was all going so much more easily than he had imagined. "Your mother said that you are from Boston. Were you born there?"

Grant shook his head. "I was born in New Orleans, sir, but as soon as my mother was able to travel, my grandfather took my mother and me to Boston to live with him. He said New Orleans wasn't a good place to raise a boy."

"I daresay he was right. Was your father a native of New Orleans?"

"No, sir. My father was an English gentleman who had come there on business. That's one reason I was glad to move here, since this is my father's country. Even though I never knew him, I can feel a little closer to him here."

"Yes, I can understand that," said Wintergreen thoughtfully. "I should imagine he would be glad that you're here, and that Mr. Channing is helping you with your education."

Grant grimaced. "I know it's not grateful of me, sir," he said confidingly, clearly feeling that he had found a friend in their guest, "but my lessons with Mr. Channing are boring and a little bothersome."

"I can understand how lessons can be boring," Wintergreen replied, puzzled, "but I'm not certain how they would be bothersome."

"He asks so many questions," said the boy, pushing

his dark hair back out of his eyes with a gesture so like Edward's that Wintergreen had to look away for a moment. "He is always asking me something about my mother."

"Perhaps it is just that he is interested in the two of you," Wintergreen suggested, but Grant shook his head.

"He likes Mother, I know that, but he seems to want to know everything about us, and I don't like that."

"That's understandable," said Wintergreen, rising from the settle. The boy was extremely observant, and he would have to tread with care. "What do you say to walking out to the stable with me to check on my cattle?"

Grant's face lit up, and he promptly forgot his grievances against his tutor. "Can we, sir? Oh, that would be better than anything!"

The chance to see the bays up close appeared to make up for the troubles of the morning, and Wintergreen showed him how to curry them, leaving Grant working blissfully as he strolled back to the inn. Because of the bays, currying had become a sacred act for the boy.

"Your son is a fine young man," he remarked to Mrs. Stanwick as he reentered the taproom, where she and Grainger were conferring over the list of supplies to be ordered for the bar.

"Thank you, sir," she replied gravely. "I do agree with you. I consider myself a fortunate woman."

Wintergreen's eyebrows rose at this. If she were so fortunate, he thought to himself, would she be petitioning him to improve her situation? Or was it, perhaps, a case of a mother wanting the best for her son?

During the afternoon, the rain grew colder and turned to sleet, peppering the windows of the inn as

Wintergreen sat cozily by the fire, ignoring Beast, who slumbered peacefully beside him, and enjoying his comfort. Or at least he did until a bedraggled Joseph came limping into the taproom, gasping for breath.

"What's the matter, Joseph?" asked Grainger, hurrying from behind the bar to help the old man to a chair. "Let me get you a tot of brandy to help you."

Joseph waved his hand feebly. "No time, no time!" he gasped. "Run for the missus!"

Grainger ran, and Wintergreen walked over to the old man, concerned by his ashen countenance.

"I'll get you the drink myself," he announced, walking behind the bar and pouring it.

Joseph drank it down gratefully, warmed by the brandy's fire.

"Now," said Wintergreen, drawing his own chair closer to the old man's, "just what is amiss, Joseph?"

Joseph, recognizing one of the quality, moreover one of the quality that was intimately involved in the problem, said, "The boy's gone, sir—and gone on one of your bays."

Wintergreen stood up abruptly. "He can't handle a horse like that!"

Joseph shook his head. "I don't know what possessed him, sir—except that he's horse mad and always has been. Being so close to them must have been too much for him."

"Is anyone looking for them?" Wintergreen demanded. "This weather is the very devil! The horse could go down and break his leg!"

"I know it, sir! Don't I know it! I think he must have started out before the rain changed to ice! He'd never have done anything that might harm the animal! The grooms are out looking for him now!"

"I'll go myself!" said Wintergreen, striding toward the door. "Which way should I ride, Joseph? Have you any idea?"

"I'd say east, sir, across the meadows. The boy always goes that way when he has the chance."

Across the meadows! All it would take would be a single hole and they'd go down! Wintergreen ran toward the stable, oblivious to the need for any gear for himself. He had almost finished saddling the remaining bay, when the stable door swung open and the boy entered, leading a limping horse.

Seeing him, Grant flinched visibly, but he led the horse into his stall and then turned to Wintergreen. "I'm ever so sorry, sir. He isn't badly injured—I think the cut on the left foreleg is a small one. We went down on an icy patch."

Wintergreen saw the cut on the horse's leg, but he also saw a bright smear of blood on the side of the boy's face. "Go to the house and have your mother look after your own hurt" he commanded.

"Not until I've taken care of the horse, Mr. Harding." He had begun to remove the saddle carefully and was speaking gently to the horse.

"I'll do that myself!" snapped Wintergreen. He could tell that Grant was having trouble remaining on his feet, and he looked for all the world like Edward after an escapade.

"I'll do it," replied the boy firmly, thinning his lips against the pain and taking a towel to dry the horse.

"Grant! Thank God you are home safely! What in heaven's name were you thinking?" exclaimed his mother, rushing into the stable with Joseph and Grainger hard on her heels.

"I just wanted to see what it felt like to ride a horse like that," he replied, continuing to wipe the horse down carefully. "I didn't intend to have him out on the ice or to hurt him."

"Hurt him? Have you hurt the horse?" demanded Joseph.

Grant nodded briefly. "Look at his left foreleg, Joseph," he said.

The old man bent down and examined it carefully while the others watched him anxiously. "It's cut, sure enough, but it'll mend. It'll need a poultice, though, so it don't swell or leave a mark. I'll fix it up right away." And the old man bustled off toward the kitchen.

Grant sighed in relief. "If Joseph says he'll be all right, he will," he told Wintergreen. "No one is better at caring for horses than he is."

"Then you had better go and take care of yourself," Wintergreen repeated, "before you fall over and we have to carry you in."

Seeing the other side of her son's face, Mrs. Stanwick took his arm and hurried him toward the door, stopping only to speak to her guest. "I do apologize, Mr. Harding. If there is any harm done your horse, we will pay for a replacement, I assure you."

Wintergreen nodded, not wishing to tell her that the price of a matched set like the bays would be greater than the sale price of the inn. Watching Joseph, however, he was inclined to believe Grant, and to leave the horse in his capable hands. Patting the old man on the shoulder, he hurried back to the inn, turning up his collar against the sleet.

Dinner was quiet, and a subdued Grant went up to bed at an early hour. Only a few of the hardiest locals made their way through the storm to sit by the fire and tell their stories, but Wintergreen placed himself comfortably in the corner and enjoyed the amusement of listening to them.

As one tall, rawboned rustic made his way into the taproom, his teeth still chattering with the cold, he was suddenly assaulted by Beast, who sprang upon his shoulder from a high shelf by the door.

There was a roar of laughter from the three other men. "So, Beast got you properly this time, McDowell!" exclaimed one middle-aged man, red-faced with the cold and the ale and his laughter. "I suppose that'll teach you to try to outsmart that cat!"

McDowell plucked the cat from his shoulder with surprising good nature and just set him down upon the settle.

"Give us a bit of paper, Grainger," said McDowell, laughing. "Let's put the cat through his paces."

The others joined in and Grainger tossed a bit of paper, wadded into a ball, to McDowell.

"All right now, Beast," said McDowell. "Are you ready?"

At this odd behavior, Wintergreen sat up a little straighter and watched the play being enacted. To his surprise, McDowell tossed the paper ball straight toward the cat, and Beast batted it back to him with his paw. There was a roar of approval from the others.

"Way to show him, Beast!" said the red-faced man, laughing again. "Don't let him call your bluff!"

On the next toss, McDowell acted as though he were going to toss it to Beast's left, then changed to the right at the last moment. Nonetheless, Beast promptly swatted it back to him, again to the approval of the onlookers.

"Have you ever seen anything to equal it, sir?" demanded the red-faced man of Wintergreen.

Wintergreen shook his head, smiling. "No, I've never seen a cat entertain itself in such a way."

"Beast is a clever animal," said Grainger. "He's always been able to do that—and he loves it. If no one plays ball with him for a while, he'll come in here and bother me until I take the time to do it."

Wintergreen watched in amusement as the cat continued his performance through the rest of the evening. Beast took periodic breaks for refreshment and naps, but he returned regularly for his next game, and the customers happily obliged him.

Wintergreen stood with Mrs. Stanwick as she locked the door after the last customer at closing time. Together they looked out over the ice-covered garden and fields, sparkling in the moonlight like a fairy-tale landscape.

"And so, do you like your work, Mrs. Stanwick?" he asked her idly, watching her as she shot the bolt into place.

"If you are asking whether I planned to keep an inn, I would say no, Mr. Harding," she replied, smiling. "But if you are asking whether I like my life here, I would say that I do. I keep a good inn and I work for honest wages, so I consider myself very fortunate."

"But a woman like you—" he began, then stopped abruptly. That was not what he had intended to say, although he had been thinking it. A woman like Marguerite Stanwick had no business keeping a common inn and being at the beck and call of people who were clearly her inferiors in manner and education.

"A woman like me must—as must many other women—earn her way in the world," she replied, finishing his sentence with a smile. "And I am fortunate. I have a way to do so while taking care of my son. What more could I ask?"

What indeed? he wondered. She seemed so sincere that it was disturbing to think she was capable of being duplicitous. In fact, he told himself, perhaps something was amiss with all of this letter business. Perhaps she had not meant what she had written—perhaps she had written them in a fit of depression over her circumstances.

To his surprise, she turned to him and smiled warmly. "It is kind of you to concern yourself about my welfare, Mr. Harding," she said. "And it was kinder still that you did not upbraid Grant for doing such an outrageous thing. I assure you that tomorrow morning when he is feeling more the thing, he and I will be having a heart-to-heart conversation about the way he must behave."

"Don't be too hard on him," Wintergreen said, leaning toward her. "I had a brother who was very much like Grant. In fact, I might almost have thought that your son was his twin if they were nearer in age."

"And is your brother wild about horses too?" she asked, her smile deepening so that, drawn by it, he leaned closer to her.

Wintergreen shook his head. "He was, once upon a time. He has been dead for many years, however."

Her smile faded. "I am sorry to hear it," she replied gravely. "I know what it is to lose someone you love."

He watched her, troubled by the evident pain in her eyes. Not only pain for the loss of her father, he guessed, but for Edward, long dead and gone as well. Strange that she should feel the loss yet still trade upon Edward's memory for gain.

As he looked into her eyes, however, he forgot Edward for the moment and leaned closer still. Despite himself, he was attracted to her as to no other woman he had ever met. The warmth of her smile and her compassion for others drew him. He was so close to her that he held his breath, then softly kissed her. When she responded, he drew her close and kissed her firmly, for a moment blotting out everything except her presence and his desire.

Abruptly, he pulled away, not allowing himself to look at her. Sternly, he told himself that he needed to remember the manner of woman with whom he was dealing and not to allow himself to be softened by such behavior. Actions, as always, spoke more loudly than words.

He bid her good night and took himself to bed, accompanied by Beast, who still appeared to have designs upon his boots. He ejected the cat twice, but when he awoke the next morning, the cat was curled in the hollow behind his knees, snoring gently.

"Well, at least you didn't awaken me by pouncing this morning," Wintergreen remarked, ejecting Beast once more from his bed. "That was good of you."

He regarded the cat judiciously. "I do think, however, that you should spend more of your time with your own family members and less with me. I'm certain that you know just how I feel about you."

Beast studied him with an unblinking golden gaze, then leapt back onto the bed and made himself a nest among the covers. Sighing, Wintergreen gave up the struggle and went back to sleep. It was much too cold to get up anyway.

When he awakened again, the fire was crackling in the grate and Beast had been removed—probably by young Grant, who would have no illusions as to whether or not Wintergreen wished for the cat's company.

When he made his way down to breakfast in the taproom, he paused before entering, remembering McDowell's fate the night before. He slid cautiously into the room, but his pains were not necessary, for Grant and Beast were seated before the fire, practicing Beast's rapid volley. The cat was much too absorbed to have time to victimize anyone. Amazed, Wintergreen watched as they batted the ball back and forth five times without pause.

"I believe he was meant for a life in the circus," remarked Wintergreen, easing past them to a comfortable spot by the fire.

"He could do it," replied Grant confidently. "I've never seen another cat to equal him—nor has anyone else who's ever been to the Golden Lion. I've often wondered who taught him how to do it."

"You didn't teach him yourself, then?"

Grant shook his head, the hair tumbling into his eyes again, and once again he swung it back with Edward's familiar gesture, avoiding the patch that covered the cut on his forehead.

"Was Beast at the inn when you moved here?" inquired Wintergreen. "Or did he come along after you arrived?"

"Oh, he was here, sir. Everyone hereabouts knows Beast."

Wintergreen nodded. That much had indeed been evident. Although he hadn't known that Beast had lived at the Golden Lion before Marguerite and Grant Stanwick, it had been abundantly clear to him that everyone indeed knew Beast.

"Come now, Grant. Time for your lessons."

Grant, Wintergreen, and Beast all turned to look at the speaker. Clarence Channing stood stiffly in the doorway, surveying the scene in the taproom with a coolly disapproving eye.

"Your servant, Mr. Harding," he murmured, bowing slightly. "Grant, leave the cat and come along with me to the book room."

Grant had lifted Beast and tucked the cat under his arm, but at Channing's words, he set Beast back on the floor.

"I understand that you gave your mother a shocking fright yesterday evening, young man," observed Channing, attempting unsuccessfully to be both familiar and disapproving. He looked down at the boy with a patronizing glance, then patted him on the head. "You should be more considerate of her."

"Yes, sir," replied Grant, flushing and avoiding Channing's eye. Grant knew that he was in the wrong, of course, but Wintergreen could see that he resented the man's words, obviously feeling that Channing had no real right to reprimand him. He hurried from the taproom without waiting for his tutor.

"A firm hand is all he lacks," Channing said to Wintergreen. "There's no real harm in the boy, but Mrs. Stanwick allows him too much freedom. He lacks discipline."

Wintergreen could see that Channing would very much like to provide that discipline. Thinking of Edward, he longed to make his feelings known to this upstart vicar who thought he could discipline Edward's son.

"I daresay his father will provide it for him when he returns," observed Wintergreen, quite as though he had no knowledge of the fact that Mrs. Stanwick was a widow.

Channing stared at him in surprise. "His father is dead," he responded. "Mrs. Stanwick has been a widow for the whole of the boy's life."

"Has she indeed?" inquired Wintergreen blandly.

"I did not realize you didn't know." He paused a moment, then added, "I am certain that, as a man of the world, you appreciate the difficulty of Mrs. Stanwick's situation."

"I should imagine that being a widow and rearing a son must always be difficult," replied Wintergreen.

"Yes, but that is not what I had reference to," said Channing, somewhat ruffled by his listener's failure to follow his meaning. "You must see that running an inn is not a suitable situation for a gently bred woman like Mrs. Stanwick, nor is this a proper place for her to rear her son."

Wintergreen, who held precisely the same sentiment, heard himself disagreeing. "It appears to me that they are both very happy here—and Grant especially seems pleased with his life."

"You saw how he misbehaved yesterday afternoon—taking your horse without permission and endangering both of them. It was only by the grace of God that they were not both badly injured—or worse!" Channing stared at Wintergreen as though he had taken leave of his senses.

"But they were not," returned Wintergreen calmly.

"Through no fault of Marguerite's—Mrs. Stanwick's, that is," the vicar added hurriedly. "He knew there would be no consequences for his misbehavior, so he felt free to do as he pleased. She does not set limits for the boy and enforce them."

"And I suppose you would," said Wintergreen, growing irritated. It mattered not at all that he had thought much the same thing himself. He refused to range himself with a narrow-minded man like Channing.

The vicar flushed and drew himself to his full height—which brought him only to Wintergreen's shoulder.

"Indeed I would," he replied. "Mrs. Stanwick knows that, and she values my views."

"And yet she did not call upon you to handle the matter for her, did she?" asked Wintergreen.

Channing looked chagrined. "That is only, I think, because we have not yet had adequate time to talk the matter over. I am certain that when we have, I shall be asked to take young Grant in hand. As I said, he needs only a little firmness."

"From what I have seen of Mrs. Stanwick, she is perfectly capable of providing any firmness she thinks necessary," said Wintergreen dryly, remembering her forceful defense of the old woman at their first meeting. "I believe you would find yourself in deep waters if you presumed upon your position."

Channing flushed an unbecoming shade of lobster red, bowed, and hurried from the taproom in search of his charge.

"Thank you, Mr. Harding," said Mrs. Stanwick. "Although I am in need of no defense, I appreciate your willingness to take up the cudgels on behalf of myself and Grant."

"I am well aware you have no need of assistance, ma'am," he replied, bowing in surprise. "I did not realize you were in the room."

She smiled. "I was in the pantry where Grainger keeps our supplies," she said, indicating a door beside the bar. "I could tell that Mr. Channing was also unaware of my presence."

Wintergreen grinned. "He was already looking as

blue as megrim by the time he went in for their lessons. If you had trimmed his sails for him, I doubt that he would have been able to do any teaching today."

"He had certainly already done an adequate amount of preaching, at any rate," she observed, "so I daresay he has expended all of the wind he had stored."

She paused a moment, then looked at him directly and smiled warmly. "It was very good of you to defend us, Mr. Harding," she said.

To his amazement, Wintergreen felt as though he were growing dizzy. Looking into her eyes absorbed him to such an extent that he wasn't certain where he was putting his feet, and he heard a sharp yowl and an angry hiss as he stepped on Beast.

To his relief, that broke the spell, and he tore his eyes from hers to look down at the cat.

"My apologies, Beast," he said, bending over to pat the smooth orange head.

In reply, Beast hissed again and swatted at Wintergreen's hand angrily.

"I don't believe he wishes to accept your apology," observed Mrs. Stanwick, amused.

"I see that," responded Wintergreen, regarding the cat with a wary eye. "I believe my best bet for a peaceful afternoon is to put Beast into the book room with Mr. Channing and Grant. Will you help me, Mrs. Stanwick?"

She looked at him for a moment, and he again had the sensation that he was drowning in eyes like the sea. "I believe that you will need it, sir," she said.

She put her hand gently on his, and he froze. "I will pick up Beast," she said. "He is accustomed to me, so he won't be so inclined to struggle."

She removed her hand, but he still felt its warm pressure. Disgusted with his own schoolboy fancies, he shook his head to clear his mind, as though he could shake out all thought of her, then turned to regard Beast. Or at least he thought he was the one doing the regarding. Beast returned his stare with intensity.

"I think it's just as well you're taking him, ma'am—and hopefully removing him from the opportunity of doing me damage," he replied, trying his best to behave normally instead of like some moonstruck halfling who had never before seen a pretty face. "I wouldn't put it past that cat to be plotting vengeance."

With a feeling of relief he watched the two of them leave the taproom, and he settled himself before the fire, prepared to set his thoughts in order. It was certainly a good thing that he had not brought Sperling along, he thought dryly. He shuddered to think of the exhibition he had been making of himself over Marguerite Stanwick. Sperling would never be able to regard his employer with the same respect after seeing him lose his composure in such a manner. And all over a pretty face and a pleasing manner!

All such thoughts soon fled, however, for the door to the taproom opened again, and he felt his heart lift when he saw her enter and smile. She lifted her empty hands.

"You are quite safe now, sir," she said lightly, seating herself beside him on the settle. "I cannot guarantee your future safety, I fear, for Beast has a long memory, as any of our regulars will tell you. Still, for the moment, he is assisting Mr. Channing by dozing on Grant's Latin lesson."

Wintergreen smiled, picturing the tutor's chagrin at such interference with his work. He knew that Channing would be irritated, too, by the fact that Mrs. Stanwick had not remained in the book room. If he knew that she had come back out to engage one of her customers in conversation, that would doubtless be the final straw for him.

"You are smiling, sir," she observed, studying his

face. "Is it because you take pleasure in having foisted the cat unto someone else?"

"Most certainly," he replied, stretching his feet comfortably toward the fire and preparing for what he hoped would be a long chat. "And thinking, too, of how happy I would have been at Grant's age to have someone interfere with my Latin lesson."

"Were you not an avid scholar, then?" she asked. Wintergreen was keenly aware that she was still studying his profile, and he was pleased to think that she seemed drawn by him, even though she knew him only as James Harding, Esquire, instead of Trevor Stanwick, Earl of Wintergreen. And even though she had so clearly not been drawn to him upon their first meeting.

"Not at all," he assured her. "In fact, I was generally considered a hopeless case. All that I cared to do was to fight against Bonaparte. My dreams were all of horses and battle and honor."

"Were they, indeed? And did you pursue those dreams? Did you join the army?"

He nodded, turning to look at her. "I did." The conversation was not following the path he had determined for it. He had planned to question her, to draw from her as much information about her past as possible. And yet here he was, rattling on about himself, like some self-absorbed schoolboy.

"And has it made you happy?" She studied him seriously, as though his answer mattered to her, and he thought about her question. Not for years had he considered whether he was happy. Not, in fact, since the hey-go-mad days when he had run away and joined the army—before Edward's death and his return to the confines of life as Lord Wintergreen.

"It did," he answered carefully. "I was, perhaps, happier then than I have ever been."

"Why did you not stay in the military?" she asked curiously, then flushed and rose quickly. "Forgive me,

Mr. Harding, for inquiring into your affairs. I did not intend to pry."

"You weren't," he said, taking her hand and pulling her gently back to the settle. It was a familiarity he knew she would not usually allow, and he was cheered by the fact that she sat down quietly and seemed prepared to spend more time with him.

They sat in comfortable silence for a few minutes, both of them staring into the leaping flames.

"My husband had a brother that fought with Wellington in the Peninsula," she said finally. "He was just such a one as you say you were. According to Edward, his life was all horses and soldiers from the time he was a boy."

Delighted by the ease with which the conversation had turned to the subject that interested him most, he remarked casually, "I served with Wellington myself—at least for a little while."

"Perhaps you knew him, then," she said eagerly. "His name was Trevor Stanwick and his father—and Edward's—was the Earl of Wintergreen."

Wintergreen shook his head slowly, watching her all the while. Her bright expression faded, and she smiled a little ruefully.

"It would have been a rare chance, of course," she remarked, "but it would have made me happy to have had such a connection. I remember clearly how dearly Edward loved his brother."

"No doubt his brother returned that affection," remarked Wintergreen a little stiffly. He did not wish her to think that the love had been all one-sided.

"I suppose so," she replied, apparently a little doubtful. "Edward thought so at least."

"And whatever happened to the brother?" inquired Wintergreen in what he hoped was a casual tone. "Do you hear from him? Is that why you returned to England?"

She shook her head, no glimmer of a smile on her

lips or in her eyes. "Edward may have been wrong about the strength of his brother's affection," she remarked, staring into the fire. "Once he became Lord Wintergreen, he appeared to have no interest in Edward's death or in his wife and child. I daresay he did not find us worthy of notice."

For a moment Wintergreen was so angry he could scarcely speak, but he forced himself to take a deep breath and to speak calmly. The woman had no notion what she was saying! She appeared to believe that the title had meant more to him than did Edward when nothing could have been farther from the truth!

"That is a strong accusation," he replied evenly. "Why do you say such a thing, ma'am?"

"I merely observe what is true," she said simply, holding out her palms face up as she spoke. "When Edward died and I wrote the news to his father, there was no reply. A letter was enclosed to be sent on to his brother, Trevor, for at that point we did not know how to reach him."

She turned her face to the fire. "There was never any answer from either of them. Edward was buried in New Orleans, and that took every cent we had in the world. If it had not been for my father returning to us as soon as he had the news, I daresay his would not have been the only death. I had very little will to live."

"Had you no one with you until your father came to you?" he asked, touched by the sincerity of her tone despite himself.

She nodded reluctantly. "My sister Marilee."

"And was she of help to you?"

Again she nodded. "Marilee was very young, however, only thirteen. Our father had left her with Edward and me while he prepared a home for them in Boston."

"Even though she was young, she must have been a comfort to you," he observed gently.

Mrs. Stanwick shrugged. "I suppose so. At any rate, she did what she could under the circumstances."

This struck Wintergreen as a rather callous dismissal of her young sister's efforts, and he looked at her curiously. "And what of your sister now?" he asked, thinking of how grateful he would be now if Edward were still with him. "Are you close?"

There was a perceptible pause. "Marilee is dead," she said in a low voice.

Wintergreen had the grace to look uncomfortable. "I'm sorry to intrude into your private affairs," he said. "I hope that you will accept my apology, Mrs. Stanwick."

She nodded and returned her gaze to the fire. After a few moments, Wintergreen gave up his opportunity to question her, and together they sat in an almost companionable silence, looking into the flickering flames.

That comfort ended soon enough, for Beast entered the room with a hiss, once again wrapping himself around Wintergreen's boot so that removing him required the joint efforts of Mrs. Stanwick and Grant, who arrived just after his pet.

"Really, Beast!" exclaimed the boy. "Mr. Harding will think you have no manners at all!"

Since Wintergreen did think precisely that, he was at a loss for an answer, but Mr. Channing, who was watching the scene with cold disapproval from the doorway, remarked, "You should not keep an animal like that at all, Mrs. Stanwick. I have told you time after time that it should be done away with."

All the others—excluding Beast—stared at him.

"How dare you say such a thing!" exclaimed Grant furiously, his face scarlet. "He is not your pet, and you have no right to say such a thing!"

"I have the right of one who is concerned about your welfare, Grant—and that of your mother," replied

Mr. Channing gravely, obviously unmoved by the boy's anger. "The cat is nothing but trouble for her."

"I assure you, Mr. Channing, that Beast is a problem that I can take care of myself," returned Mrs. Stanwick, still attempting to pry the cat loose from Wintergreen's boot.

"So I see," responded Channing dryly, bowing briefly. "I must go now, for I have other duties that must be attended to, but I am certain that you know I am always at your service. Should you decide to do the reasonable thing about the cat, I shall be happy to take charge of the matter."

And, bowing once more, he turned and left the taproom.

"Of all the nerve!" exclaimed Grant. "Did you hear what he said about destroying Beast?" One final effort released Wintergreen's much-abused boot from the last claw Beast had embedded in it, and cat and boy tumbled backward onto the floor. Grant clutched the annoyed cat firmly to his chest and looked at the others.

"He just doesn't understand how you feel about Beast, Grant," said Mrs. Stanwick comfortingly. "He sees the cat only as a problem."

"He sees Beast as a problem to himself," replied Grant bitterly. "He thinks that Beast interferes with my lessons and with his being able to pay attention to you."

Grant paused for a moment, thinking, and his eyes lit up with amusement. "Do you remember his face when Beast leapt off the mantel onto his shoulders? He was leaning over your hand to kiss it, and Beast almost knocked him on his face! Scared the liver out of him!"

Wintergreen saw with satisfaction that Mrs. Stanwick was hard pressed not to laugh at the memory. He himself would have enjoyed seeing that happen, he reflected. The complacent vicar must have had his self-esteem badly damaged by that encounter.

The evening passed pleasantly enough. There was a crowd in the taproom, for a midday thaw had improved the weather, and Wintergreen enjoyed watching the locals in their ongoing sparring with Beast. It was clear that the cat enjoyed the contests as much as they did. He had no doubt that Channing would be hard pressed to find a single person present who would agree with his suggestion that Beast be put down. Even McDowell, who was most often Beast's target, enjoyed the give-and-take of the struggle, and his admiration for his foe was obvious.

Wintergreen planned to leave the Lion the next morning to return to London, but he had been unable to decide upon his course of action. Originally, he had planned to reveal his identity to Mrs. Stanwick before he left, and to indicate to her just why she had best write no more letters importuning him about her son. Now he had no idea what he would do—except that he would certainly provide for Grant.

However, he no longer felt as absolutely positive as he had that Edward had not indeed married Marguerite Stanwick. She was certainly not the type of woman to establish a liaison outside of marriage, no matter how discreet the arrangement. Nonetheless, he had received no letter from Edward through their father, and no such letter had been found among his father's effects. Nor had he mentioned a marriage. All that Wintergreen had heard of had been Edward's death.

"What are you thinking about so seriously, Mr. Harding?" asked Mrs. Stanwick, seating herself beside him. "You were laughing at Beast, then suddenly your laughter stopped and you looked as though you were thousands of miles away."

"I suppose I was," he replied, smiling a little. How could it be so comfortable to be talking with this woman? He had not liked her at all when he first encountered her upon the street in London. He had thought her a handsome woman but scarcely an appealing one. And if she had indeed been Edward's wife, could it be right to be so drawn to her?

She studied his face a moment, then put out her hand and touched his cheek lightly.

"I did not like you at all when I saw your behavior in London," she remarked, unconsciously echoing his own thoughts. "I thought you arrogant and cold."

She smiled, and he had the now-familiar sensation of drowning as he looked into her eyes.

"I'm afraid that I was doing what my father always accused me of—leaping to conclusions," she confessed. "I was mistaken about you."

Wintergreen moved uncomfortably. "I am not so certain that you were," he said. "In truth, I didn't notice the woman who was knocked down by the beggar, and I don't believe I would have thought to stop if I had noticed her."

"I don't believe that," responded Mrs. Stanwick firmly. "I believe that you underestimate your own kindness. Just look at your reaction to Grant's taking your horse. You did not abuse him as so many men would have done when he brought the animal back injured. And you were preparing to go out into the storm yourself to find them."

"He was injured himself," said Wintergreen, "and he took the responsibility for his own actions. He did not try to lay the blame elsewhere. That is a rare quality in anyone—let alone a mere boy."

"Yes, he is always forthright," agreed Mrs. Stanwick. "That is one of his most endearing qualities. He has been a great pleasure to me. I shall hate to send him away to school, but I suppose that I must. Mr, Channing tells me that will be necessary soon."

Wintergreen reflected that Mr. Channing would undoubtedly like to send Grant away to school if he could fix his interest with Grant's mother, but he did not give voice to the thought.

"Did Grant travel to London with you?" he asked. "Is that what you were doing there, looking at schools?"

Mrs. Stanwick shook her head. "I had other personal business there," she answered simply, and the silence that followed informed Wintergreen that she had no intention of elaborating upon the statement.

Business there! With an unpleasant start, he remembered the second letter that had been delivered. Undoubtedly, that had been her business. But how, he wondered, could he reconcile that action with the woman who sat beside him now?

He turned to look at her, trying to banish the letters from his mind, and she was gazing at him, both of them oblivious to anyone else in the room. The last customers were filing out of the room, with Grainger following them to bar the door. Beast had disappeared, undoubtedly to take up residence upon Grant's bed, where he slept each night.

"A penny for your thoughts," she murmured as he drew closer.

"Someday I shall tell you," he responded in a low voice, pulling her to him and kissing her. Just when that would be, and what the thoughts would be, he could not tell himself. For the moment it was enough that they were there together.

He held her tightly, his face pressed against the fragrance of her dark hair, until they heard Grainger returning from the front door. Then she gently slipped from his arms and straightened her gown, turning to speak to the waiter as he entered the taproom.

"Well, Grainger, how cold is it tonight? Will our customers get home without a chill?"

The waiter grinned at her. "McDowell and the others have enough warmth to keep them for a mile or two," he replied. "I believe the quantity of porter they drank can hold the cold at bay. And the ice is still melting in great puddles."

"I believe that I, too, must take my leave tomorrow," Wintergreen said reluctantly, pained by the look of surprise on her face as she turned back to him. "If the ice is gone, I must be on my way."

"Must you, indeed?" she responded absently, twisting a fold of her gown in her hand. "We shall miss you—particularly Grant and Beast, of course."

"I shall miss you all," he said simply, "but I shall be back soon to see you."

"Of course you will," Mrs. Stanwick replied, forcing a briskness into her tone and manner that he knew was not genuine. "We shall look forward to it. We always encourage our customers to return, do we not, Grainger?"

"Indeed we do," he agreed, looking from her to Wintergreen. "I shall tell Joseph to have your rig ready in the morning, sir."

"Thank you," said Wintergreen, realizing that he had been relegated to the status of customer rather than friend. "I shall see you in the morning, ma'am," he added, bowing to Mrs. Stanwick before leaving the room.

"Of course you shall," she returned brightly. "We shall set you on your way with a hot breakfast. We do not allow our customers to leave us hungry."

As he made his way up the stairs, he was surprised by the sudden emptiness he felt. She had shut the door upon him as firmly as though there had been a real one to close between them. She was the innkeeper, he the good customer. They were no longer anything more than that. He wondered if she had hoped to capture Mr. Harding, an obviously wealthy man, as her next husband. Certainly Mr. Harding would be a better catch than the vicar—and perhaps she had decided that there would be help forthcoming from the Earl of Wintergreen.

* * *

Sleep was long in coming that night, and by the time it came, he was no nearer a decision as to what should be done about the problem of Marguerite Stanwick than he had been earlier in the evening. Indeed, the clarity with which he had seen the matter before meeting her seemed to him a faraway dream.

Morning brought no enlightenment, but neither did it bring Beast, he noted gratefully. He was able to pack his things quickly, ready to return to London as soon as he had his breakfast. He grimaced at his top boots as he pulled them on. Appelby was never going to understand. His valet, he knew, would already be deeply affronted because he had not been allowed to accompany his master, but to bring home his boots in tatters would be the final blow to Appelby's peace of mind.

Wintergreen walked briskly down the stairway, each step waxed to a gleaming brightness that sparkled in the morning sun. Unaccountably, he felt his spirits rising. There would undoubtedly be a way to work things out and at least to provide for the boy. If Marguerite Stanwick was the proper minister's daughter she presented herself to be, all might be well. If she was not—here Wintergreen shrugged—if she was not, he would cross that bridge when he reached it. He had faced difficult challenges before.

So absorbed was he in his own thoughts that he did not notice the shadow above him as he reached the landing to make the sharp turn to descend. When Beast dropped upon his shoulder from the railing several feet above him, Wintergreen was completely unprepared. He was knocked off balance and his foot shot out from under him, sending the pair of them hurtling down the steps to the stone floor below. In an instant of blinding clarity, Wintergreen saw the iron doorstop in the shape of a crouching lion, and knew that he was going to hit it.

He awakened slowly to an overwhelming sensation of throbbing. At first he was hard pressed to locate its source, but finally he traced it to his head. Feebly, he raised his hand to see what the difficulty was, but he felt someone take his wrist.

"There'll be none of that, sir," said a brisk and unfamiliar voice. "You'll do yourself more damage if you go poking about like that."

Painfully, Wintergreen managed to open his eyes and focus upon the speaker. A portly man with gray hair and a trim gray mustache was regarding him with an air of ownership.

"I just got those stitches in place, sir, and I don't want you to be messing about with them."

"Stitches?" repeated Wintergreen groggily, not quite taking it in. "You took stitches in my head?"

"Ten of them, sir, and neatly done, too, if I do say so myself. I told my wife just the other day that I am as neat a seamstress as she is herself."

Here he held up a looking glass to Wintergreen so that he could admire the handiwork that had been done on the side of his forehead.

"You took quite a nasty blow to your head when you hit that lion, sir. You were fortunate to have no more stitches than you did."

Memory began to filter back to Wintergreen, and he winced as he remembered the vision of the lion as he had tumbled toward it.

"Well, if ten stitches is all that it cost me, I suppose I am a fortunate man," he returned.

The surgeon regarded him with an approving eye. "Indeed you are, sir. You could have had a very nasty blow. As it is, you have only your stitches and your splint."

"My splint?" said Wintergreen, startled. "What splint?" he asked, trying to raise his head from the pillow to inspect himself.

"Now, just you lie perfectly still, sir," remonstrated the surgeon. "You broke your right leg in the fall, and I've set it very neatly. If you go twisting about, you'll overset all my good work and cause yourself to walk with a limp, for the bone won't heal properly."

Wintergreen collapsed back upon his pillow. It only needed this, he thought. Now he was trapped here, a prisoner of the surgeon and Beast and Marguerite Stanwick. For a brief, wild moment, he wondered if she had arranged the whole affair so that she could finally get what she wanted for her son.

Then he remembered that Beast had also gone tumbling down the steps with him—and he remembered the boy's fondness for Beast.

"How is that blasted cat?" he asked the surgeon.

"Beast is all right, sir," said a small voice from the far side of the bed. Wintergreen had not yet looked in that direction. Just moving his head was an agony. "And I am so sorry, Lord Wintergreen. He's never been responsible for really hurting someone before."

"Come here where I can see you, Grant," he commanded, and the boy moved slowly into his range of vision. Wintergreen could see that the boy had been crying, although he would deny it, of course.

In spite of his anger with the cat for causing this, he could not bring himself to rail at the boy. Instead, he heard himself saying, "I slipped on the steps, Grant. It was not actually Beast who was responsible for my fall." No one had actually witnessed the episode, so who could correct him?

The boy's face brightened. "Really, sir? It wasn't Beast? I thought most certainly that he had done it, for he was standing beside you when we ran in after we heard the crash. Mr. Channing said that certainly Beast had finally killed somebody."

"What a charming sentiment," commented Wintergreen dryly, thinking to himself that Mr. Channing was certainly not the most compassionate individual he had encountered. "I suppose he was saying that over my broken body instead of trying to help me."

"My mother told him to go home if he was not going to be of help," Grant said. "She stopped the bleeding and had Grainger send one of the grooms for Mr. Watley."

"And she very wisely did not move you until I arrived," added Mr. Watley, the surgeon. "She had covered you with blankets, but she would not let anyone do anything else. You should be very grateful to her, sir."

"Of course I am," replied Wintergreen absently, his thoughts busy in another direction. Grant had called him Lord Wintergreen. That had just made its way through to his consciousness. How had he come to know his name?

"Is your mother here?" he asked. "I should like to thank her myself if she is."

Grant nodded and hurried from the room.

"I should like to speak with Mrs. Stanwick alone," Wintergreen said to Mr. Watley, who was hovering at the foot of the bed, eyeing his patient with a proprietary air.

"Of course, sir—but it should be a brief visit," he added. "You need your rest."

He passed Mrs. Stanwick as she entered and gently closed the door behind him. Mrs. Stanwick approached the bed slowly, Wintergreen noted grimly, without a single glance at him.

"May I be of some assistance, Lord Wintergreen?" she asked coolly, her eyes directed at a point several feet above his head.

"I wish to thank you for your help, Mrs. Stanwick," he replied. "I understand that you were responsible for taking care of me after my accident."

"You are welcome, sir. I would have done as much for anyone to whom that happened."

"I believe you," he said, smiling a little. And he did. It would not have mattered whether the victim were friend or foe, guest or stranger, Marguerite Stanwick would have helped.

Silence settled over the little room. She had had him placed in her own chamber, the only one on the ground floor of the inn. The furnishings were simple and spotless, as he would have expected them to be.

Finally, abandoning hope of her saying anything more, he asked, "May I inquire how you came to know my identity?"

"Do you mean how I discovered that you are not Mr. Harding but the Earl of Wintergreen, Edward's brother?" she asked, still not looking at him.

"After your accident, I took the liberty of looking through your things to see if your direction was there, or the name of a relative, so that we could notify someone of your accident."

"I see. And what did you find?"

"This," she said briefly, removing a folded letter from her pocket and handing it to him.

He took it reluctantly, recognizing a note he had written to Sperling and not yet sent. His name was upon it, as was his seal.

"May I ask, Lord Wintergreen, just why you are here, and just why you were here under a false name?" She still avoided looking at him, and her voice was as filled with starch as her cook's white apron.

She was the picture of wounded dignity, Wintergreen thought, angered by her pretense of innocence.

"Just what would you have had me do?" he demanded. "Given the outrageous requests that you were making of me, what would you have me do differently?"

"Outrageous requests?" she asked, staring at him

blankly. At least, he thought with satisfaction, that had caused her to look at him directly.

He nodded. "I received your letters, Mrs. Stanwick—if that is indeed your name—demanding that I recognize your son as the true Earl of Wintergreen."

If Wintergreen had thought her eyes stormy at their first encounter, he discovered his error. He had now stumbled into hurricane waters.

"I wrote no such letters!" she exclaimed. "How dare you accuse me of doing such a thing—and how dare you doubt my very name!"

She turned sharply, but before she could reach the door, Wintergreen called to her, "Tell me this, then, Mrs. Stanwick. If that is truly your name, and you were truly my brother's wife, describe for me the birthmark on his right shoulder!"

He saw with a sickening drop of his heart that he had stopped her cold. She turned and stared at him a moment, then left, closing the door behind her silently.

She did not know! Edward had had a curious brown birthmark, almost in the shape of a star, on his right shoulder. His wife would certainly have known of it, but Marguerite—whatever her last name might truly be—Marguerite knew nothing about it.

He stared at the ceiling, puzzling over the matter. What, then, of the boy? Most certainly he was Edward's child. And, if he were indeed a love child, why would Marguerite not know of the birthmark?

A sharp pain washed over him as he tried to move his leg, and it was morning once more before he was once again conscious of the world around him. A deep rumbling informed him before he even opened his eyes that Beast had taken up residence upon his bed, and the warmth against his left side informed him of the cat's precise location.

"I cannot escape you, can I?" he asked, opening his eyes and staring down at the cat. Beast's eyelids flickered in recognition, and he reached out a paw to swat lazily at Wintergreen's shoulder.

"Wonderful! Now that I am bedridden, you are moving in for the kill, are you not?" he inquired dryly. To his amazement, however, Beast did not rise to pounce upon him. Instead, he maintained his purring and burrowed against him.

"I do hope that you are comfortable, Beast. I should hate to think that I'm putting you out in any way."

"Would you like me to move him, sir?" asked Grant, easing through the door with a tray of food. "I would have done so before, but he seemed to want to sleep with you instead of me last night. My mother was sitting up with you, and she said that Beast did nothing but lie there and purr."

"Your mother sat up with me, did she?" inquired Wintergreen. "That was thoughtful of her."

"She feels responsible, you see," explained the boy confidingly. "Between the stairs and Beast, she is certain that we are at fault for your accident."

"You may set her mind at rest, Grant. I do not plan to take any action against her because of my accident. She need not worry about that."

Grant looked shocked. "Oh, that isn't why she is distressed, Lord Wintergreen. She is just sorry that you had this happen."

"Indeed?" commented Wintergreen. He was touched by the boy's belief in his mother, but his own experience with people had made him far less trusting. Undoubtedly, the innkeeper feared that he might wish for her—at the least—to pay for his expenses. "Would you ask your mother to come in to see me?" he asked.

Inexplicably, the boy colored deeply and murmured, "I believe she is very busy just now, sir. Perhaps a little later in the day she might be able to come in."

"She won't come, will she?" asked Wintergreen, and the boy shook his head.

"If you'll forgive me, Lord Wintergreen, I must go

down for my lessons now, but I'll be up as soon as Mr. Channing leaves."

Left to his own devices, Wintergreen eyed the cat, who returned his gaze unwinkingly. "Well, what shall we do to pass the time, Beast?" he inquired.

Glancing about for some amusement, he saw on the table at his bedside the letter that Marguerite had taken from his satchel. Reaching for it, he tore off a bit of it and scrunched it into a ball. Beast recognized the preparation and moved toward the end of the bed, raising himself onto his hind legs so that he would be in swatting position.

"Here we go, Beast!" said Wintergreen grimly, tossing the paper ball to the cat, who promptly bounced it back to him.

The long afternoon was spent in the same manner, with Wintergreen tiring long before Beast did. Finally, Wintergreen lay back against the pillow and slept, the cat firmly ensconced at his side, both of them snoring.

When Wintergreen awakened, twilight had filled the room, and only the flickering of the fire lighted it. On his bedside table was a stack of what appeared to be Grant's school papers, and on top of it was a note from the boy, inviting Wintergreen to use them as paper balls for Beast, since he had seen the evidence of their play. Wintergreen grinned and the play resumed once more. After another hour of play, however, he once again grew weary. More than anything, he wanted to talk to Marguerite Stanwick.

Infuriated by his own helplessness and even more by Marguerite's refusal to come in and speak with him, he finally managed to get himself out of bed and into his dressing gown. His valet arrived at this moment, having received Marguerite's message about the accident, and he returned Wintergreen to his bed, assisted by the surgeon, who had also just arrived.

"Indeed, you must do this, sir, or you will end up

without the proper use of your leg if you persist in trying to walk upon it."

"I see, sir," said Appelby impassively, "that I have arrived just in time. Given a few more hours and you would undoubtedly have crippled yourself for life. I have often told you that you should not travel without me."

Growling, Wintergreen called for stationery and ink and a pen.

"Indeed, sir? Turning literary rather late in life, aren't you?" inquired Appelby. He had served the Stanwick family for most of his days, and the liberties he took with his master would have startled the rest of the servants if he had revealed them.

"Just bring the damn things to me, Appelby!"

"Very good, sir. Since you put it so persuasively, I shall do so," the valet said agreeably, withdrawing in search of the required items.

When Grant appeared with a tray bearing Wintergreen's supper, he handed the carefully written note to the boy. He had not apologized for his behavior in the letter, but instead had demanded that she come to him so that they could complete their conversation.

"Hand this to your mother for me, will you, please, Grant?" he asked.

Grant nodded and disappeared rapidly, leaving Appelby staring at his master.

"Well, what is it, Appelby?" demanded Wintergreen sharply.

"It would be quite enough for me to hear you use a civil tone of voice with a common serving boy in an inn, my lord. That would be adequate to put me to bed for a week or two—but it's the boy himself, sir. Did you not look at him closely?"

"Of course I did, you idiot! Why do you think I am here?" replied Wintergreen crossly.

"Ah, I recognize your manner now, sir," responded Appelby. "And I cannot blame you for it, for it is so very like seeing Master Edward again that I can scarcely credit my eyes."

"Well, credit them," said Wintergreen briskly. "And when his mother arrives, leave us alone, please." Appelby did as he was bid, bowing her into the room. For a moment he stood outside the door, feeling that he had stepped back in time some twenty years.

Inside the chamber, Marguerite Stanwick glared at Lord Wintergreen. "Just why did you come here?" she demanded. "Are you here just to spy on us? And how did you know we were here? We have been living at the Lion for two years now."

Angered by her deceit, he replied sharply. "I am here because of your letters, just as I told you! Quite naturally, I wished to see for myself what manner of woman you are."

"And have you seen?" she responded, stung by his tone as well as his words.

"I have indeed! Were it not for my blasted leg, I would be gone from here in an instant!"

"And that would not be too soon for me!" she assured him. "Coming in here and trying to make love to me simply to extricate information about Edward! I can see that you are nothing at all like your brother, who was truly a gentleman!"

She turned to open the door before he could respond, but she stopped and turned back slowly toward him. "I shall not tell you again that I did not write those letters, for I know that you will not believe me. But I should like to know myself just who the writer was."

Wintergreen stared at her. "Just what proof do you have of Grant's legitimacy?" he demanded bluntly.

Marguerite's color rose, but otherwise she showed no reaction to his words. "There is no official record," she replied slowly, "so you may rest easy, Lord Wintergreen. Your title is quite safe."

"This isn't about my title!" he returned sharply.

"Indeed?" she asked. "I think that is exactly what this is all about. You are afraid that Grant will take your place."

Wintergreen all but ground his teeth in response. He had thought about this likelihood long ago, and had determined in his own mind that if Edward had had a child, he could have deferred to that child without any problem. Indeed, he would have taken it upon himself to see that Edward's child received every benefit due to him; therefore, to have such a woman hint that he was acting out of selfish motives was unendurable.

"Not at all, ma'am," he managed to reply with creditable calmness. "Have you no proof at all that you were married? No record, no witnesses?"

"My father married us," she replied shortly. "And he is dead."

"But you must have had a record of it," said Wintergreen. "A license? What of your own marriage lines? Or a witness?"

Marguerite shook her head, more reluctantly this time. "My sister was the only witness that we knew; the others were acquaintances of Edward's. As I told you, Marilee died. As for our marriage lines—"

Here she shrugged again. "The paper is gone," she said simply.

"Gone?" asked Wintergreen blankly, staring at her intently. "How could it be gone?"

"I have no idea," Marguerite returned grimly. "After you told me of the letters you received, I sat at my desk in the book room and carefully went through my papers. I would suspect someone of stealing it, but it could be of value to only a few people—to me—and to Grant, of course. And to you," she added quietly. "It is gone, as well as the record of Grant's birth."

This observation, of course, did nothing to improve his frame of mind. "Well, I certainly don't have either of them!" he said bitterly. "A fine thing to say, ma'am!

To be sure, I wander about the inn at night, searching through your private papers. Just a little too convenient to lose them now, wouldn't you say?"

"I did not say that I only just lost them," she observed thoughtfully, "but, as a matter of fact, that is true."

She stared at him for a moment. "As you just noted yourself, Lord Wintergreen, it seems quite convenient that someone would take them now, wouldn't you say?"

Before he could make an angry rejoinder, she took from her pocket a small box and presented it to him. "Perhaps you might recognize this."

Wintergreen drew an emerald ring from the box. "Yes—this belonged to my mother," he said quietly.

She nodded. "Yes, that is what Edward said when he presented it as a wedding ring."

"Why do you not wear it?" he asked abruptly. "Do you no longer consider yourself married?"

"Of course I do!" she snapped. "But wearing such a ring isn't suitable for me now."

"I should imagine not," he responded dryly. "No doubt it is more convenient to allow the gentlemen who stay here—particularly the wealthy men like Mr. Harding—to think of you as an eligible widow."

Marguerite stiffened as she snatched back the ring and placed it in the box. "I had thought you might be a man of conscience," she replied, her cheeks flaming. "I understood that Edward loved you and considered you an honorable man. I see that perhaps he did not know you as well as he had thought."

"He knew very well that I was no pigeon for the plucking," said Wintergreen, his expression growing bleaker. "He would have left proof of your wedding. He would have known that I would expect that—or every third child on the street could be presented at my door as Edward's child."

"Perhaps he did not plan for his child to become

an earl," she said calmly, watching him. "Perhaps he thought that such a life was not what he would want for his son."

Startled that she would say such a thing, Wintergreen could only stare at her for a moment. "I see that you have quite different plans, however," he said finally. "Perhaps my brother would not thank you for that."

"Perhaps he would not," she admitted, still determined not to repeat her statement that she had not written the letters, "but I do not think he would thank you either. You seem to care nothing for the welfare of his son."

As Marguerite left the room, Appelby reentered it, wisely maintaining his silence after a glance at Wintergreen's stormy countenance. As the evening wore on, however, he managed to engage his master in conversation, gleaning what details he could about the situation. It was clear to Appelby that something would need to be done about the boy, but since Wintergreen's indisposition confined him to the inn, the valet decided that there was time enough for matters to work themselves out.

Boredom overwhelmed Wintergreen during the next few days. Grant came to visit him now and then, but Mr. Channing seemed more intent than ever upon keeping him busy with his lessons, and Wintergreen was forced to spend most of his time with Beast. He acquired a small mountain of paper balls, and the two of them practiced hour after hour, until Wintergreen began to see paper balls even in his dreams. They were everywhere—on the counterpane, on the bedside table, scattered across the floor, on the windowsill.

Late one afternoon, he had Appelby gather them all up for him, and he spent an idle hour smoothing out the balls and amusing himself with the bits and pieces of writing he found on them. There were lines from cookery books, occasional scraps of letters, and lists, and finally—to his amazement—a record of the marriage of Edward Stanwick and Marilee Masters. There were two signatures for the witnesses, and one of them was that of Marguerite Masters.

Thoughtfully, Wintergreen put the paper in the pocket of his dressing gown and decided to bide his time. Just what this meant he was as yet uncertain, but surely a little more time might reveal a few more pieces of the puzzle.

He and Beast returned to their sporting pastime, for the cat spent hours with him. He had been forbidden entrance to the book room during Grant's lessons, and the boy felt quite certain that Beast was sorry to have played a role in Wintergreen's accident, and that he was trying to make amends for that by providing entertainment for his guest.

"Perhaps you are right," replied Wintergreen in amusement. "At the very least, he seems dedicated to keeping my aim accurate."

"I think that he is lonely too, sir," observed Grant thoughtfully. "Now that he isn't allowed to come with me, he has no one to spend his time with and he is a little out of sorts. He is a great deal like you, Lord Wintergreen."

Here he realized the liberty he was taking and flushed, but Wintergreen did not appear to take it to heart. Appelby, however, who was inspecting the wreckage of his master's boots, looked up sharply and inspected the expressions of the other two.

After the boy had left, Appelby ventured to say, "He grows more like Mr. Edward every day, my lord."

Wintergreen nodded without speaking.

"And, if I may say so, sir, over the years you have grown more like your late father."

Astounded, Wintergreen wheeled to stare at his

valet, and Appelby braced himself for the onslaught he expected.

"What the devil do you mean by that, Appelby?" he demanded. "What a lot of poppycock! I am no more like our father than Edward was!"

"You were not much like him when you were a boy," said Appelby, "but as the years have gone by since you came home from the war, I have seen you change more and more."

"My father was a cold, uncaring man!" exclaimed Wintergreen. "He gave no thought to anything or anyone that did not serve his own interests!"

Appelby maintained a discreet silence, and Wintergreen continued to stare at him.

"So that's it, is it?" he said finally. "You think I have changed that much, then, Appelby?"

There was a pause, but the valet finally nodded. "In the old days, sir, you and your brother were as like as two peas in a pod, and every servant loved you both—loved you for your wild, brave ways and your kindness."

He looked at his master, and his eyes misted. "I watched the change in you after your brother died and you came home and took your father's place. One by one, you shut out everyone. You never notice any of the people who serve you, as you did when you were a boy. The lady here, Mrs. Stanwick—"

He saw Wintergreen's expression darken at the mention of her name, and he hurried on. "Mrs. Stanwick does the kind of things you and your brother did. Why, she went down to London just to bring back the sick sister of Grainger, the waiter who works in the taproom."

"She went to London for Grainger's sister?" demanded Wintergreen. "Is that what she was doing there?"

Appelby looked at him, puzzled by his reaction.

"Yes, that is what I was just telling you, my lord. That's just the kind of thing—"

"Never mind that now, Appelby! Go and get her for me! Tell her I must see her right away!"

Growing alarmed about his master's state of mind, Appelby tried to calm him, but a metal tray hurled at his head sent him hurrying in quest of Mrs. Stanwick. There were moments when Wintergreen must not be trifled with, and this was clearly one of them.

As Wintergreen waited impatiently, Grant poked his head through the open door. "May I come in, sir?" he asked.

"Yes, Grant. Do come in," Wintergreen replied, glad to see the boy and eager for anything that would pass the time. "Have you finished with your lessons?"

Grant shook his head wearily. "I don't believe so. Mr. Channing is downstairs, talking to my mother about what to do with me. I'm afraid he'll want me to translate some more of Cicero before he leaves. He wrote out one of the passages he wants me to memorize too."

Wintergreen shook his head in sympathy. "I hated that too," he said, taking the paper from the boy's hand and glancing down at the passage. "Let's see if I know any of it still."

His gaze froze as he looked at the passage.

"What is it, sir? Are you feeling ill? Should I have Mother send for the surgeon?" Grant stared anxiously at Wintergreen, who still did not move. Even in the dim light, Grant could see that he had become pale.

Suddenly, Wintergreen crumpled the paper in his hand. "Grant, run to your mother. Tell her that she might have ignored Appelby's message, but that she must come to see me immediately—and that she must bring Mr. Channing!"

Grant looked at him as though he had gone mad. "Mr. Channing?" he repeated. "Is it about my Latin?"

"Go, boy! Go!" shouted Wintergreen. "Tell her that

if she does not come this instant, I shall drag myself out of bed and crawl down the passage if I must!"

Truly alarmed now, Grant sprinted from the room in search of his mother. In less time than it took Wintergreen to regain his composure, he had reappeared with his mother and Mr. Channing in tow, and Appelby hovering anxiously in the background.

"What is it, Lord Wintergreen?" asked Mrs. Stanwick crisply. "You have frightened Grant out of his wits. What is this all about?"

"I believe that my conversation should begin with Mr. Channing," replied Wintergreen, eyeing the vicar, who moved uneasily under his gaze.

"With Mr. Channing?" she asked in astonishment. "Do you wish to know about Grant's studies? Is that what all of this is about?"

"He is a very poor scholar," said Channing nervously. "I have done the best that I can for the boy, although it is rather like trying to make a silk purse out of a sow's ear. He has no talent for his books at all."

"A silk purse out of a sow's ear?" interrupted Mrs. Stanwick, glaring at him. "Is that the way you refer to Grant? I don't believe I shall be requiring your services any longer, Mr. Channing."

Mr. Channing looked at her desperately. "Now, Mrs. Stanwick, pray don't be rash. You must take a more sensible view of the boy. You should send him away to school—"

"I don't wish to go away to school!" said Grant. "I want to stay here! Why should I wish to go somewhere without horses?"

"You see," said Mr. Channing to Mrs. Stanwick. "He has no sense of proportion. Unless he plans to be a stable boy, there is no sense in allowing him to spend so much time with horses—"

"Gentlemen spend a great deal of time with their horses," said Wintergreen quietly.

Mr. Channing laughed thinly. "And what would that have to do with Grant?" he asked. "Certainly you do not fancy that he is a gentleman!"

Wintergreen nodded. "I do," he said. "I feel quite certain that he is Grant Edward Stanwick, Earl of Wintergreen."

Everyone in the room stared at him.

"And we have you to thank for drawing this to my attention, Mr. Channing," he continued smoothly, seeing that everyone else was too startled to respond.

"Me?" the vicar squeaked, running his finger around his collar as though it had suddenly grown too small for him. "What do you mean by this madness, sir?"

"Had you not written to me, pretending to be the boy's mother, I would have had no notion of his existence, so you see, you have done me a great favor."

*"You* wrote to Lord Wintergreen?" demanded Mrs. Stanwick, turning upon the vicar. "How did you have any information that would make it possible for you to do so?"

The vicar backed away from her nervously, still pawing at his collar. "This is really a most unfortunate misunderstanding, I assure you, Mrs Stanwick—" he began.

"May I ask, ma'am, just where you keep your private papers?" Lord Wintergreen interrupted.

"Why, in the bottom drawer of my desk in the book room," she responded. Then, as she realized what she had just said, she stepped closer to the cowering Channing. "Do you mean to say that you opened my private letters and read them?" she asked in disbelief.

"Only a few of them," he said. "I read only enough to give me some idea of the boy's identity, and I thought that perhaps—perhaps if he were out of the way so that you were free to give your attention to someone aside from the boy—"

"You thought I might be interested in you?" demanded Mrs. Stanwick, disbelief written vividly on her face. "In *you?* Is it possible?"

The expression on the vicar's face was ludicrous. "Well, yes, it did seem to me that you were far too involved with the boy to allow for a healthy relationship with a man. I could have done much to—"

"You could have done nothing, for even without Grant I would have had nothing to do with a man like you! A man who would read my private letters!"

"I read only a few of them," protested Channing feebly, still clinging to hope.

Here Wintergreen beckoned to him to come closer to the bed. Channing approached nervously, and Mrs. Stanwick followed him, curious to hear what Wintergreen would say.

Wintergreen lowered his voice confidentially, and Channing leaned even closer to catch what he was saying.

"You should have read more of those letters, Mr. Channing," he confided.

"More of them?" said Channing nervously, beads of perspiration forming on his forehead as he glanced back at Mrs. Stanwick.

Wintergreen nodded. "If you had, you would have known that this is Marguerite Masters, Grant's aunt, rather than his mother, Marilee Stanwick."

"His aunt?" repeated Channing feebly.

Wintergreen and Marguerite both nodded. "Grant has always known that," she said. "After Marilee died several years ago, he started calling me Mother, and when we moved here to the inn, I decided that it would be better for a widow to be an innkeeper than it would for a spinster."

"A judicious decision," agreed Wintergreen. "One that I wish I had realized earlier."

He turned to Channing, who looked as though he were suffering from a severe case of shock. "Did you by any chance, Mr. Channing, carry away some of

Mrs. Stanwick's—excuse me, Miss Masters's—private papers with you from the book room?"

Channing nodded miserably. "The other day," he admitted, "the boy came into the room just as I had taken some out, and I stuffed them under his school papers."

Wintergreen looked at Marguerite. "I fear that Beast and I unwittingly used some of them for sport. We will need to find all of them and press them flat once more, my dear."

Marguerite smiled, although she appeared to be ignoring the "my dear." Turning toward Mr. Channing, she said coldly, "I believe, sir, that it is more than time for you to take your leave of us."

Miserably, Channing crept out the door, Appelby stepping to one side to allow him passage as though he were the victim of a loathsome disease. Catching Grant's eye, the valet grinned and motioned toward the door. The boy nodded in understanding, and the two of them silently left the room, closing the door gently behind them.

"You realize, Marguerite, that I am at a severe disadvantage," Wintergreen observed, looking up at her tenderly. "I should be able to go down on my knees to ask your forgiveness, but I cannot even manage to go down on one."

She appeared to consider the matter for a moment, then seated herself on the side of his bed. "I accept your makeshift apology for the moment," she said thoughtfully, "but when your leg is mended, I shall expect one properly delivered."

"You shall have it," he assured her. "Just as you shall have proper recognition of Edward's son."

"But I was not the one who was demanding it," she reminded him, smoothing his hair back from his forehead in what he considered the most comforting manner imaginable.

"But I am the one who shall see to it that Edward's

son receives his title," Wintergreen answered. "In time I shall grow accustomed to not being an earl."

"And will it be such a difficult matter, giving up your title?" she inquired.

He shrugged and grinned boyishly, pulling her closer to him. "Perhaps I am more like Edward than I had realized," he confided, kissing her. "It is possible that I may even marry into the same family."

Suddenly, an orange ball of fur dropped upon them from the headboard of the bed, crumpling the immaculate cravat that Appelby had so tenderly arranged.

"This is not an opportune moment, Beast," announced Marguerite. She picked up Beast carefully and walked him to the door, opened it, placed him on the floor outside, and closed the door firmly.

As she reseated herself on the edge of the bed, she smiled at Wintergreen and tenderly smoothed his rumpled cravat and his tumbled hair.

"And now, my dear, where were we?" she inquired gently.

"I believe I remember," he murmured, once again folding her in his arms and looking into the sea depths of her eyes. "And may I tell you that our wedding trip will be on a ship, my dear? I have always loved the sea."

At the door Beast yowled plaintively, but neither of those in the chamber even heard him.